Peter Potts

Other books by Clifford B. Hicks

THE MARVELOUS INVENTIONS OF ALVIN FERNALD

ALVIN'S SECRET CODE

ALVIN FERNALD, FOREIGN TRADER

ALVIN FERNALD, MAYOR FOR A DAY

FIRST BOY ON THE MOON

THE WORLD ABOVE

Peter Potts

by CLIFFORD B. HICKS

E. P. DUTTON & CO., INC. NEW YORK

For Bayneeta and Cathy—
with love unexpressed

Published simultaneously in Canada by Clarke, Irwin & Company Limited, Toronto and Vancouver

SBN: 0-525-36945-7 LCC: 76-133118

Designed by Dorothea von Elbe
Printed in the U.S.A.
First Edition

Contents

1

This Chapter Tells About an Accident with a Hornets' Nest, and Two Very Important Things I've Observed About Life.

Lots of times, I've noticed, you get in trouble by accident, when you're trying to do something perfectly good and useful.

Just take last winter. We were studying nature at school.

"Bring in any plants or insects you can find this time of year," said Miss Gillam. "You may have to dig under the ice and snow to find them."

Those were her very words. Who'd think anybody could get in trouble just by following his teacher's instructions?

Up under the eaves, by my bedroom window, was

a hornets' nest that had been there for a couple of years. I pried loose the ice, got down the nest, and brought it to school. I figured an insect house was almost as good as insects.

At first Miss Gillam thought it was fine. She passed the nest around the room so all the other sixth-grade kids could see it. I was sitting in the back row, and when the nest finally came around to me, I put it on the floor under my desk.

It's not my fault that Miss Gillam had given me a seat by the radiator. And I *didn't* kick that nest under the radiator on purpose.

Now, I can't think like a hornet, so I can't tell exactly what happened. I suppose, though, that when the radiator gave those bugs a hotfoot, they thought it was spring. Anyway, all of a sudden I saw about a dozen hornets staggering out from under the radiator, like they'd just been wakened out of a sound sleep.

I won't even try to tell you what happened. Even now, my stomach gets fluttery just thinking about it.

Joey Gootz's ear swelled up as big as a baseball. Joey is my best friend. Minnie Shugelmeyer got so sick she had to stay home for a week. Both the Aldrich twins got stung three times on top of both heads. I don't mean each of them has two heads. They each got stung three times. You wouldn't think hornets could count, would you?

Worst of all was Miss Gillam. She was just bending over to straighten up the books on the bottom shelf in the back of the room. She got stung twice.

I suppose it's pretty tough for a teacher to stand up all day. It certainly wasn't *my* fault. But to hear her talk, you'd think I *aimed* those hornets. Besides, I think it made her mad that they didn't sting me.

That's a good example of what I mean about getting in trouble by accident.

Another thing I've noticed is that people treat you just about the same way you treat them. If you treat them mean, they'll treat you mean right back. If you do them a favor, they'll break their necks to do something for you.

That's the way Pop feels too, and he's a good example of what I mean. Betts and I are lucky to be living with him.

Pop isn't really my father. He's my grandfather, but everybody in Fairfield calls him Pop, so I do too. Betts and I came to live with Pop and Grandma six years ago, when our folks died in an auto accident. Three years later Grandma took sick and died too, so that left only Pop, and my older sister Betts, and me. We live in Pop's old farmhouse on the edge of Fairfield, which is a small town, but maybe the best one in the whole world.

Our house is just outside the city limits. It used to be a handsome farm, but it's pretty run-down now. The barn folded up in a puff one night when Pop was hobbying with secret formulas. Pop hobbies all the time since Grandma died. He doesn't farm anymore, but earns some money doing odd-job carpentry around Fairfield.

Betts, who is nineteen, raises chickens and sells women's clothing at McClennan's Department Store. She doesn't raise the chickens at McClennan's—just sells the clothes. She's also in love. I have two paper routes and dig up odd jobs whenever I can, fifty cents an hour.

A good example of people treating you the way you treat them is Joey Gootz. Joey has been my best friend for a zillion years, and the only fight we've ever had was once when he fell out of a tree on my head and I thought he did it on purpose. But Joey and I do lots of things for each other.

Like when he helped me pull that loose tooth—which is another time I got in trouble by accident.

2

Good Ways to Pull a Loose Tooth, Requiring Only Some Fishline, a Live Chicken, and a Barbell.

The first time I noticed the tooth was last June, late one afternoon. I'd been helping Joey put up some fence posts around his backyard. His dad had been after him for a week to get them in, and was madder'n a rooster without any tail feathers because Joey hadn't done it. I had given Joey a hand. It was an afternoon that would bake a potato, and I was tuckered out by the time I headed through our front door.

I eased into a three-point landing with my head on one arm of the easy chair, my legs on the other, and my in-between between. Pop and Betts were talking in the kitchen.

Did you ever notice that the first time you discover a loose tooth you get a strange feeling, as though your body is coming unglued? The tip of my tongue happened to hit this tooth, and something wobbled. I thought my head was coming off. I reached in with my thumb and forefinger and could taste the Gootz mud on them. The tooth wiggled a little when I pushed. I knew then what it was.

"Pete, will you set the table?" Betts was standing in the kitchen doorway. "And how about taking your dirty hands out of your mouth?"

"Wumpppfff!" I said, around my finger and thumb. "Loose tooth."

"Here, let me see."

Betts came over and knelt by the chair. Sometimes she acts like she's my sister, and sometimes like she's my mother. It's a little confusing, but mostly I like it.

She wiggled the tooth, and I reared back. You learn pretty early in life that a loose tooth is your own personal property, and you don't want anybody else messing with it.

"Pete, I think you're in trouble with that tooth."

Something clattered in the sink out in the kitchen, and Pop came walking in. He was frowning, which gave him even more wrinkles than usual. He has a long skinny face with wrinkles that cut every whichway across it.

"What's wrong?" Pop must have heard what Betts said.

"Pete has another tooth coming in behind this one,"

said Betts. "It's coming in crooked because this one isn't out yet. Pete, that can be pretty serious."

"Wait'll I get a pair of pliers," said Pop, heading for the door.

"No!" I squealed. I jumped out of the chair. "Nobody touches that tooth but me!"

Well, we had a pretty big argument about it. Betts and Pop kept telling me that if the second tooth came in crooked I'd have to live with it that way the rest of my life. I kept waggling the tooth with my tongue and telling them that nobody was going to touch that tooth but me.

Finally Pop laid down the law. "Pete, I'll give you until day after tomorrow. If that tooth isn't out by noon Thursday, I'll personally haul you in to Doc Jenkins and have him yank it right out of your head. Now, go set the table."

In bed that night I began worrying about the tooth. Doc Jenkins is a nice guy—he always buys from us kids when we set up a Kool-Aid stand—but I didn't want him poking his big tools in my mouth and grabbing my tooth. Besides, I knew it would cost money, and we didn't have any to spare.

I made up my mind that no matter what happened I was going to pull the tooth myself the next day.

I didn't sleep very well.

The next morning, I waited until Pop and Betts left for work. Then I got out my fishing pole and cut off about three feet of fishline. I tied a slipknot in one end. It took me a good ten minutes to snag it up tight around that loose tooth, but I finally managed to do it. The line tasted a little bit like an old catfish, but I didn't mind.

By then I guess I was pretty tired, so I sat down and read a chapter out of my library book. It was so exciting I read another chapter. All that time, though, I had this nagging *thing* in the back of my mind, like when you get a stone in your shoe. Finally I put down the book and looked out the window. The sun was shining on the trees out front, so I went outside and sat down on the front steps.

I consider myself naturally pretty brave, so it was very strange when I discovered that *I couldn't pull that string*. I'd grab the string in both hands, take up the slack, and then feel the tooth wiggle as I applied pressure. But at that instant I'd always back off.

I just couldn't pull it.

It was then that Joey came riding over on his bike. He sat down beside me without saying a word, which is natural for Joey. He never says much, and lots of times, when he does talk, it isn't in sentences, but in ideas. And he has some wild ones.

Joey is a little bigger than I am, and has kinky red hair. When he was seven years old he got his nose broken by a steam shovel while they were building the new gym, so his face looks a little flat in front.

Finally he said, "Why the string?"

I told him about the tooth, and how I had to get it out myself or go to the dentist.

He looked at the string. "Jerk it," he said.

"I can't." I hated to admit it, especially to Joey, but he seemed to understand.

"Want me to?" he asked, reaching for the string.

I flipped the string out of his reach in a hurry. I reminded him what a private thing a loose tooth is, and how every kid has the right to pull his own. Nobody should pull a tooth except the kid whose mouth it belongs to. Nobody should even ask to *waggle* somebody else's tooth.

Joey sat there and nodded his head in agreement. Finally he said, "An accident would be okay."

"What do you mean?"

"Well, if you didn't know *when* it was going to be pulled, and a *thing* instead of a *person* pulled it, then it's just as good as you pulling it yourself."

For Joey, it was a long speech. I thought about it for a while, and what he said made sense to me too. "Okay. How do we do it?"

"Doorknob," he said, standing up and heading inside.

He took me through the living room and into the kitchen. He closed the door between the two rooms, put a chair right in front of it, and shoved me into the chair. He reached for the string but I wouldn't let him have it. Not on your life.

"Tie it," he said. "Doorknob."

I tied the loose end good and tight around the knob. After he'd inspected the knot, Joey walked out the back door, whistling as he went.

Naturally I knew what he planned to do, even

though he hadn't explained it to me. He'd walk around to the front of the house, sneak into the living room, and jerk open the kitchen door. It would be the door that pulled the tooth, not Joey, so everything would be okay.

He whistled for a while out in the backyard, taking his time so he could surprise me. It was a pretty good plan. There wasn't much that could go wrong, and the tooth would be out in a hurry. The more I thought about it, the better I liked it, until suddenly I noticed that I wasn't hearing his whistle any longer. That began to bother me, and when I heard a squeak from the loose floorboard on the front porch, I could feel the sweat begin to roll down my forehead.

It probably didn't take Joey more than thirty seconds to sneak across the living room to the kitchen door, but it seemed like three hours to me. I was holding onto the seat of the chair, but it was all I could do to keep from grabbing the string.

By now I'd focused my eyes on the doorknob. I've never been hypnotized, but now I know exactly how it feels. Everything around the knob seemed to blur and disappear into a blob, so all I could see was the knob itself. It was an old knob, like everything else in the house, and there were two little dents right in the top that I'd never noticed before.

That knob began to turn!

I don't even remember moving, but I must have leaped out of the chair and hurled myself at the door, trying to keep it from opening. It had opened just a crack by the time I hit it full force. There was a loud *crunch* from the other side as I barreled through the doorway, barely managing to grab the knob, swinging around with the door.

"Ooooowwrrrfff!"

The sound came from the floor of the living room. Joey was lying there on his back, both hands covering one of his eyes. As fast as I could, I untied the string from the doorknob and knelt down beside him.

"What happened?" he asked.

"I got hypnotized by the doorknob," I said. "You were on the other side of the door when I came slamming through. Are you hurt?"

Joey groaned. He took his hands away from his left eye. The edge of the door had really clipped it. Already it had swollen almost shut and was beginning to turn purple.

"Tooth?" he asked after another groan.

I had to tell him that we'd misfired. I got an ice cube from the refrigerator, helped him to his feet, and we went outside to sit on the steps. He held the ice cube against his eye to cut down the swelling and the throbbing.

Every once in a while Joey would look over at me and grin, even though that eye must have hurt like fury. Then he began studying the string that still dangled out of the corner of my mouth. Joey and I know each other so well we can almost read each other's minds, and I knew he was trying to figure out another way to pull the tooth.

"Chicken!" he finally exclaimed. He threw away the ice cube and stood up.

Well, it was a typical Joey Gootz idea, because it showed a great deal of imagination. I could see the possibilities right off, as soon as he said that one word.

We headed back to the hen house where Betts keeps her chickens. She has a regular egg route set up to make extra money, and everybody in Fairfield says her eggs are the best in Jasper County.

Joey and I stood by the fence around the hen house, looking over the prospects. Finally Joey pointed at a big leghorn that was like an egg factory as far as Betts was concerned. She produced eggs on an assembly line. The hen, I mean, not Betts. She was one of the heaviest hens in the coop, and Betts's favorite. Betts had named her Henrietta.

"Okay," I said to Joey, "let's catch her." I had doubts, though, about what Betts would say if she caught us disturbing Henrietta.

He opened the gate and walked inside, still holding a hand over his sore eye. A chicken isn't the easiest thing in the world to catch. Joey gave a terrific leap through the flock, trying to reach Henrietta, and it was like a bomb going off. Chickens exploded in every direction, some of them flying up into Joey's face. I saw one of them hit him in the swollen-shut eye, so I ran into the coop to help.

We pinned Henrietta in the corner of the fence, and Joey lunged for her. He managed to grab one leg, and she squawked like fury, scratching away with her loose foot and pecking at his arm. By the time he had her quieted down, his shirt was ripped in two places, and blood was trickling down his wrist. He looked pretty bad, with that eye puffed out and blood on his arm, but he was grinning as he walked out the gate.

Joey climbed across some old fence boards Pop had left in the backyard. He calmed Henrietta by clucking at her and tucking her head under one of her wings. That's a good way to calm down a chicken.

He pushed one of her feet from under her and held it out in my direction. I gulped, looking down at Henrietta's foot, but I finally screwed up my courage and tied the end of the fishline to it. I tried to get away with a pretty loose knot, but Joey made me tighten it.

When we were all ready, he sat Henrietta down on a stump and slowly backed away. I watched him, not Henrietta, because I knew he was the one who would give the signal that would pull the tooth. I was still watching him back away when he tripped over those old fence boards before I had a chance to warn him.

Well, several things happened at once.

Joey had just opened his mouth to shout at Henrietta and make her fly off the stump. As he tumbled over backward he let out a holler that could have been heard in Timbuktu.

Henrietta let go with the biggest "Squaaaaaaawwwk!" of her life, and her wings started drumming the air as she took off.

I heard the squawk and immediately knew what was going to happen. I clamped my good front teeth down on that fishline like I had lockjaw and grabbed for the string. There was a jolt that almost jerked my head off my neck, but my front teeth held, and I managed to snag the fishline with my fingers before any real damage was done.

While I was listening to Joey moan over on the fence boards, I reeled in Henrietta like she was a catfish. I sat down on the stump, and as fast as I could I untied the string from Henrietta's foot. When I finally let her go, she took off toward the hen house with a screech.

Betts never did know what caused Henrietta to ease off her egg production for a week.

I ran over to the woodpile and found Joey sprawled on his back. He was only about half conscious when I got him to his feet, and he staggered all over the backyard holding the back of his head. When I finally calmed him down enough to take a look, I could see a big lump poking out of his head, and what looked like splinters sticking out of it. He wouldn't let me touch the splinters, though.

"Tooth?" he finally gasped, looking up at me with his good eye.

I had to tell him that we'd failed again.

When he got over being dizzy, we walked around and sat down on the front steps. We looked at each other a minute and then began laughing. It must have hurt him even to laugh, because he kept rubbing first his eye, then the scratches on his arm, then the back of his head.

"Well, what are we going to do about the tooth?" he finally asked. That's one thing I like about Joey; once he starts something, he sticks to it.

I took a good look at him sitting there. He was a mess. The sight did something to me. I swear I became a new man, right then. I fingered the end of the string dangling from my mouth.

"I'm going to pull it," I announced suddenly. Even I was surprised when the words popped out.

"Really?"

I thought a long time before I answered. "Yep. *I'm going to pull that tooth myself!*"

"Well. Go ahead."

I thought again, for quite a while. "Well, I can't just pull it with my hands. But I'm going to pull it. Let me plan for a minute."

Joey wiped blood with his handkerchief while I thought. Suddenly I *knew* I had the way to pull that tooth. I jumped up. "Follow me."

I went inside, to Pop's bedroom. Scattered all around it were leftovers from Pop's hobbying.

Pop started hobbying three years ago, right after Grandma died. He said he puttered to keep his mind occupied. Since then, his hobbies have covered the alphabet—from astrology to zithers—with in-between stops for atomic energy and hamsters.

He throws himself into a new hobby like fury. When he was learning to be a sculptor, he once worked all night trying to shape five hundred pounds of clay he'd dredged up from the banks of Salt Creek into a woman wearing a sheet. When the result didn't please him, he took up weight lifting so he could "change himself from a ninety-pound weakling into a he-man." Instead of becoming Commando Tough, he sprained his back and was laid up for more than a week.

Now, on the table over in the corner of his room, I spotted his new book on hypnotism, and knew he could hardly wait to get home from work so he could get back to it. It wasn't the hypnotism book that I wanted to borrow, though. It was the old weight-lifting set under his bed.

"Help me roll it out," I said, stooping down and pointing to the barbell.

The barbell had some big weights on each end. Joey took one end, and I took the other. We toted the whole thing out into the living room and clanked it down on the floor.

Joey already could sense my plan, and his eyes—at least the open one—were beginning to shine. He knew he was about to see a display of raw courage.

First I tested to see if I could lift the barbell off the floor alone. It was heavier than a sackful of dead muskrats, but I managed to lift it a couple of inches off the floor, then lowered it again. I figured that, with a superhuman effort, I could get it up as high as my chest.

I stooped over and tied the end of the fishline right in the center of the barbell.

"Okay," I said. "Stand back. I'll need plenty of room."

Joey reached over and shook my hand. "Good luck," he said. He backed away a couple of steps.

I gritted my teeth. If I was ever going to get that tooth out, it was right now. Right now, I thought, trying to screw up my nerve.

Right now. . . .

With one hand on each side of the barbell, I gave a mighty grunt and hauled upward. I figured if I could get it chest high, then drop it, there'd be no doubt that the tooth would come out in a hurry. No matter what happened, I *couldn't* botch the job this time.

I hauled upward with all of my strength, and heard about six of the bones in the middle of my back pop. My eyes were bugging out, and my legs started to shake.

Well, I got that barbell as far as my waist, and thought I'd never get it any farther. I was determined, though, to hoist it up to my chest. To tell the truth, I'd forgotten about the tooth, what with the strain on my muscles, and the challenge of trying to lift that much deadweight.

I still don't know where I got the strength. I took a deep breath. Suddenly I bent my knees and crooked my arms at the same instant. The barbell came to rest across my chest, just as pretty as you please. Now all I had to do was straighten my legs.

Slowly, straining every muscle, I straightened up. Until that moment, I didn't know that I'd made one mistake. My feet were too close together. Just as I stood up straight, I could feel the barbell sort of sliding off-balance to the left, I staggered in that direction, but went a little too far, and suddenly the barbell was tipping to the right.

I was intent on keeping all that weight under control as the barbell began to twist a little, one end swinging around to the rear. I pivoted with it, and made another big mistake. I got my left foot caught behind my right one.

By now the barbell was swinging pretty wildly, almost out of control. I staggered across the room, trying to get it balanced again. If it hadn't been for Joey, that barbell and I might have gone right through the living room wall.

Joey told me later that he saw the barbell swinging in a big circle, but that he was so excited about watching me stagger across the room he failed to notice that he was right on the edge of the circle.

I was hollering at him for help when it happened. One end of the barbell swung right around, and the weight clipped Joey across the mouth.

Joey fell backward, and I could see blood spurting out. The sight must have brought me to my senses and given me superhuman strength. That happens, you know. Our fifth-grade health book said that in times of stress you become lots stronger than you are regular. This was a time of stress, all right.

I planted my feet wide apart and steadied the barbell. Joey was groaning on the sofa, so I worked just as fast as I could. I lowered the barbell so it was across my hips. My arms were hanging straight down. Then I eased it down to the floor.

It must have taken me a good sixty seconds to untie the string from the barbell.

Joey was holding his hand across his mouth when I reached him, and blood was running out between his fingers. I pulled his hand away. It wasn't a very pretty sight. He had a big gash on his lip.

I was holding his hand in mine, and suddenly I noticed something white in it. It was one of his teeth.

That really scared me. I knew I had to get him to the doctor or the dentist, to find out how much damage had been done.

"Come on!" I said, helping him to his feet. I gave him my handkerchief. "Put this in your mouth."

He was in a daze, and I had no trouble pulling him out the front door and down the steps. His bike was handier, so I got on the seat, and made him ride on the bar.

We rode as fast as I could pedal into Fairfield. It isn't a very big town, as I said once before. Doc Jenkins and old Dr. Snyder have their offices together in a little house they bought when Mrs. Larkin moved to the city. Doc Jenkins is the dentist, and you go to Dr. Snyder for everything else.

When we got there, I didn't even bother to swing down the kickstand on Joey's bike. I just dropped the bike, and jerked Joey up the steps behind me. Scared? You bet I was.

Off to the left, I could hear Dr. Snyder talking to somebody behind a closed door, so I jerked Joey into Doc Jenkins's office. He was sitting in his dental chair. It was tilted way back, and he was dozing. In his lap was a magazine with a pretty girl on the cover.

"Doc Jenkins!" I shouted.

His eyes flew open, and when he saw Joey standing there with blood pouring into my handkerchief, he leaped out of the chair. I don't suppose the sight of Joey's closed eye, or the scratches on his arm, or the torn shirt helped, either. When he eased Joey down into the chair, Joey gave a gasp. The bump on his scalp had hit the headrest.

"Good heavens!" said Doc Jenkins, only he used different words, of course. "Must have been a *horrible* accident!"

He tried to make Joey comfortable in spite of the splinters in the back of Joey's head, then went right to work on Joey's mouth, cleaning away the blood.

For about three minutes he didn't say anything, just daubed at Joey's mouth and squirted stuff inside. Finally he turned to me. "Not nearly as bad as it looked," he said. I heaved a sigh of relief.

By now, most of the bleeding had stopped. Doc put a little bandage across Joey's upper lip, and took one more look inside his mouth. He motioned Joey out of the chair.

"That cut on your lip will heal in no time, Joey," he said. "Outside of that, you lost one tooth, but it won't be long until you get a new one anyway. No real damage done." He looked over at me. "What happened?"

Well, I told him everything. I thought maybe he'd laugh at us, but he didn't. He didn't even smile, but his eyes sort of crinkled at the corners.

Finally, when I'd finished, I asked, "How much do we owe you, Doc?" By then I was worried about where we were going to get the money to pay him.

His eyes crinkled a little more. "I didn't really do anything, boys. I just took a look at Joey's mouth, and put on a little bandage. I can't really charge you for that. Besides, it's been a slow day, and you brought in a little excitement."

He looked straight at me. "Pete, you look a little silly with that string dangling out of your mouth."

You know, I'd forgotten all about the string, I was so worried about Joey!

At that moment, Doc Jenkins reached out, took hold of the string, and gave a little twitch with his fingers. The string popped out of my mouth, and until I saw the end of it swinging through the air, I didn't even know that the tooth had popped out too! I didn't even *feel* it.

It was great to get rid of that dingblasted tooth, finally. But it had been Doc Jenkins who pulled it, and that's what he gets paid to do.

I sort of stammered out the question. "How much do I owe you for pulling my tooth?"

He screwed up his lips, as though he was thinking about the answer for quite a while. Then he said, "No charge, Pete. After all, you brought your own tools!"

3

Here's a Good Idea for a Birthday Present—Maybe.

I've never seen Joey look as sad as he did that morning. It really surprised me because it was a Saturday morning, which meant we didn't have to go to school. Furthermore, it was the best spring day of the year—a day to do something special.

When I was still half a block from Joey's house I whistled like a cardinal. He didn't come sailing out the door like he usually does. I whistled again, then sat down on his front steps and watched some ants play follow-the-leader across the sidewalk.

Finally Joey came to the door. At first I thought he

was trying to kid me, with that awful down-in-the-dumps look on his face.

"Let's hike up the creek to Springer's Woods," I said. "Either that, or go fishing. I know where there's the biggest ball of red worms in Jasper County."

Joey looked at me. There was no hope at all in his eyes. "Come on in," he said. He didn't even react to my suggestions.

Mrs. Gootz was standing by a mirror in the front hall, humming to herself while she buttoned her coat.

"Hi, Pete," she said. "Isn't it a beautiful day?"

I agreed.

"It's Mom's birthday," blurted Joey, still with a face like a hound dog.

"Happy birthday, Mrs. Gootz," I said. "Looks like you're going out to celebrate."

"You're right, Pete. It also happens to be Mrs. Filbert's birthday. Every year we celebrate together. Today we're going on an all-day shopping spree in Center City, complete with a fancy lunch."

"I hope you have a fine time," I said.

"Thanks, Pete. I'm sure we will." She looked out the front door. "There's Mrs. Filbert now. Joey, don't forget to rinse the breakfast dishes before you go out. For lunch, there's cold ham in the refrigerator. Your dad won't be back from the convention until tonight, but I'll be back late this afternoon in time to fix supper. You kids behave yourselves, now, and don't get into any trouble. Okay?"

"Sure, Mom," said Joey. "Have lots of fun." He sounded like he was delivering a funeral oration.

Mrs. Gootz leaned over and kissed him on the cheek. Except for her kissing, nobody could ask for a finer mother than Mrs. Gootz.

"Now, come out and say hello to Mrs. Filbert," she said.

My heart didn't leap wildly with joy at the prospect of seeing Mrs. Filbert, but I followed Joey out the door. I suppose Mrs. Filbert is a nice enough woman, but she's always trying to impress everyone.

We waved good-bye as they drove away, then sat down on the curb and made bird noises with maple seeds. Between chirps, I looked over at Joey and said, "What's your problem?"

"You can't help," he said in a low voice.

"Maybe I can. Anyway, get it off your chest."

"Mom's birthday." He reached in his pocket and pulled out a quarter. "To buy her a present."

"You mean that's all you have?"

He nodded.

"Well, you're right. You have a problem. That won't buy much of a present."

He sat there looking glumly down his squashed nose.

"Let's see," I said, trying to cheer him up. "Maybe she'd like some licorice whips."

Joey shook his head. "She's on a diet."

"Well, maybe we can find a cheap pair of earrings at the dime store."

"Only make it worse. Tubs."

I knew right away what he meant. Mrs. Filbert has this guy Tubs for a son, and he's in our room at school. He's not very popular with the kids, but the adults think he's terrific because he's so polite. His parents give him about a billion dollars a week for an allowance.

What Joey meant was that Tubs would get his mother something really spectacular for her birthday, like the Queen of England's prize jewels. So Joey didn't dare get his mother a pair of dime-store earrings.

Joey stood up. "I've got to rinse the dishes."

It was right then that the idea struck me, like I'd been hit on the head with a barn beam. "Wait, Joey! Listen! Why don't we both give your mother something really special for her birthday? I mean, something she would never imagine we could do?"

Now I had Joey's attention, so I went on. "Suppose we give her a complete day off, and do all of her work for her. You know. We could clean the house from top to bottom, do the laundry, even cook supper so it would be ready when she got back."

Joey thought for quite a while. Then his face blossomed into a smile. "Not bad. Impress her. And wouldn't cost a cent."

"Might be fun," I put in.

"Bake a birthday cake too! Besides, she's been worrying about getting her spring housecleaning done."

"We can do it for her!" I exclaimed. "The whole house. Clean sheets on all the beds. The whole house clean as a pin when she gets back, with a birthday cake on the table and supper in the oven."

"Let's go!" Joey headed for the front door.

We decided to do the laundry first because it would take a while to dry. We stripped the beds, picked up all the dirty clothes we could find, including a pair of Joey's old sneakers, and headed for the basement. That's where Mrs. Gootz does her laundry.

Joey dumped everything into the washer—all of the sheets, a batch of socks, Mr. Gootz's bright red shirt that he'd worn only once, and some striped towels. It was a pretty big load, and we really had to squash down the clothes in order to pack in the sneakers and some rags Mr. Gootz had been using to clean the engine of his car. We finally got everything in, though, and Joey pushed a button that let in the water and the soap flakes.

Beside the washer, on top of the ironing board, were two of Mr. Gootz's white shirts and a couple of dresses that were clean but still had to be ironed.

"Shall we do the ironing now?" I asked.

"Later. Let's air the stuff in all the closets. Mom has been wanting to do it for weeks."

We ran upstairs and attacked the closets. Armload by armload, we carried all the clothes down to the backyard and hung them on the clothesline. I was just staggering out with the last load, which included three pairs of Mr. Gootz's shoes, when Mrs. Fenneman's yellow dog from next door came moseying over to see what was going on.

Wouldn't you know, I accidentally dropped one of Mr. Gootz's shoes, and that dog snatched it up and started toward the alley with it. I knew I had to get that shoe back, so I hollered at Joey, dropped the rest of the clothes, and took off after the dog.

I never saw a dog that could run so fast. He was like a yellow bullet going down that alley, across Hickory Street, and up Route 22 toward the waterworks. I never did catch him, and finally hiked back to Joey's house.

We talked it over while we picked up the clothes out of the flower bed, where I'd accidentally dropped them in the excitement, and brushed them off. Joey said his father wouldn't mind about the shoe, that it was an old one, but I knew he was just trying to make me feel good.

"Let's check on the laundry," he said, when the clothes were all on the line.

We went down to the basement, and do you know what?

There was something wrong with that washing machine!

It was filled to the top with water, soapsuds, and clothes, but it was just sitting there sort of trembling and groaning. You'd think manufacturers could make machines that won't break down, wouldn't you?

There's a limit to my ability—and Joey's too—just like anybody else. We knew we couldn't fix that washer, so we didn't even try. We *did* try getting hold of Mr. Fulmer, who repairs things, but it was Saturday and he'd gone fishing. We finally decided we'd leave the washer just the way it was until he came back from Three Crow Pond. That way, the clothes could soak, and probably they'd be clean by the time the washer was fixed.

But I'll admit that the washing machine kind of rattled us. We somehow had a guilty feeling, as though *we'd* done something wrong, when actually it was the washer that had quit. I know it isn't logical to feel guilty when you're not at fault, but we weren't quite as enthusiastic about the work when we attacked the ironing.

"You ever done any ironing?" I asked.

"No. You?"

"No. But I've watched Betts lots of times. It looks easy to me. I don't know why women make such a big fuss about it."

Joey plugged in the iron, and we waited a couple of minutes. Finally he licked his finger and smacked it across the bottom of the iron. It sizzled good.

"What shall we do first?" asked Joey, moving the stack of clothes off the ironing board to make some room.

"Let's do one of your dad's shirts."

Joey pulled a shirt out from the middle of the stack and laid it across the ironing board. "Which end?"

After studying the shirt, I said, "Start on the bottom. That will give us a little practice by the time we get up to where it shows."

Joey stretched the shirttail across the ironing board,

and I slid the iron across it. You know, it turned out just as smooth as any shirttail that Betts ever ironed! I was surprised at how easy it was. Joey was pretty impressed too, but then he jabbed a finger out at a slanty little wrinkle right at the bottom of the shirttail.

How did I know he was going to jab a finger at that wrinkle just as I slid the iron toward it? Anyway, I ironed his finger.

Joey yowled like a dogfight, and waved his hand through the air while jumping up and down on one foot. You'd think he'd been murdered.

I finally got him calmed down enough to take a look, and there was a big blister on the end of one of his fingers. It looked pretty sore, all right, but not as sore as all the fuss he'd been making. For a kid who gets hurt so much, Joey sure yells.

"Do you have any salve?" I asked.

"Upstairs," he mumbled, sucking on his finger. "Medicine cabinet."

We both went upstairs to the bathroom. Joey found the salve. I smeared some of it over the blister while he grunted and groaned and rolled his eyes at the ceiling. I found a roll of gauze, tore off a piece, and wrapped it around the finger. Maybe I used a little too much because his finger looked like it had a snowball stuck on the end, but just the sight of the bandage calmed him down.

It was while I was wrapping a foot or two of adhesive around the bandage that Joey got a kind of funny look on his face, and began to sniff. Then I smelled it too.

"The iron!" Joey shouted, and ran for the basement stairs.

The basement was full of smoke and smelled a little like the city dump every Friday, when they burn it off. The smoke was so dense around the laundry that we couldn't even see the ironing board. Joey was a real hero, though. He vanished, just as though he'd been swallowed up. By the time I got to him, he'd unplugged the iron and set it up on its hind end, so it couldn't do any more damage.

"The windows!" Joey gasped.

Coughing and sputtering, we opened the basement windows. Within two, three minutes we could see again. I was amazed that the iron really hadn't done much damage. It had just burned a hole right down through the shirt and into the ironing board. That was all, though. No other damage. It was such a neat hole, just the shape of the iron, that I figured Mrs. Gootz could patch it without too much trouble. Just to be on the safe side, Joey dumped a bucket of water over the ironing board.

We were still coughing some, so we went upstairs, and out on the front porch to get some fresh air.

We sat there, on the front steps, our eyes watering a little. It seemed like everything we'd tried so far had gone wrong. Of course it wasn't our fault that the manufacturer had made a faulty washing machine, or that Mrs. Fenneman's yellow dog had run off with Mr. Gootz's shoe. When you come right down to it, it wasn't our fault that I'd ironed Joey's finger, either, and if that hadn't happened we wouldn't have burned the hole in the shirt and the ironing board. Still, we were feeling pretty glum. The weather wasn't helping our spirits, either.

The weather!

We'd been so busy doing all that housework that we hadn't even noticed what was happening. The April clouds had rolled in, and the sky was already as dark as it is when the streetlights come on at night.

"Hey, Joey," I said, punching him with my elbow, "we'd better get those clothes off the line before it rains."

We were just rounding the corner of the house, heading for the backyard, when the wind hit. Lots of times an April shower starts with a gust of wind, and this was a real boomer, bending over the trees and rattling the windows. It caught us from behind and blew us right on out to the clothesline. Some of the clothes already were skittering along the grass when the rain came.

Those first drops were about the size of half-dollars, so big you could see them coming. Joey and I each grabbed a big wad of clothes and ran for the house. By the time we reached the door, it had become a regular cloudburst.

We threw those armloads of clothes on the kitchen floor and ran back for more. I had to practically swim through that downpour. It took three trips to get all the clothes inside the kitchen, and at the end there was a pretty soggy lump of stuff lying on the floor.

We stood there, soaked to the skin and shivering, while we thought about our next move.

"Let's dry off," said Joey, which seemed like a sensible thing to do. We went to his room, and he loaned me a pair of pants and a sweat shirt.

Warm and dry again, the world didn't look quite so bad. We sat on the bed planning our next move.

"Those clothes have been aired out," I said hopefully. "That's one thing we've done."

"Right. Washed a little too. Probably cleaner than they were before. But wet."

"Sooner or later they'll dry out, wherever they are. Even in a closet. It's just a matter of time."

Joey thought for a minute. "Right. Let's put 'em back in the closets."

It must have taken us an hour to sort out those clothes, put them back on the hangers, and hang them in the closets. I was really proud of the job we did, though. Every one of those closets was just as neat and tidy as the clothing racks at McClennan's Department Store, even though the clothes dripped a few puddles on the floor.

By then it was about noon, and Joey's stomach was growling, so he suggested we stop for lunch. I started to get the ham out of the refrigerator, like his mother had said, when he stopped me.

"Peanut butter," he said.

I slid the ham right back in, and got out the peanut butter and made some sandwiches. I drank quite a lot of milk in order to get the peanut butter unstuck, and we finished off with some bananas. Everything looked a little better on a full stomach.

"What'll we do next?" I asked.

"Clean the living room," Joey said, looking at the bandage on his finger.

We found some rags and dusted the top of everything in the room. I never could see why women make such a big thing out of dusting. I'll bet we had the whole job done in two minutes flat.

Joey got out the vacuum cleaner. It was one of those with a cloth bag hanging on the handle. I plugged it in, and Joey began running it back and forth across the rug. Pretty soon we had a game going. I took my dust rag and acted like a bullfighter, and he'd come charging at me like a bull.

I had my eye on the bull and made an especially good move with my cape, then dodged to one side without watching where I was going. There was a little glass vase on the table, and I knocked it off. When it hit the floor, the handle broke off, and just then the bull came charging right across that area. The vacuum cleaner sucked up the handle of the vase.

There was a horrible grinding noise inside the vacuum cleaner. We both stopped the game and listened. It sounded like a hundred pairs of roller skates on a rough stretch of sidewalk.

Joey turned off the vacuum cleaner, then turned it back on. The grinding noise came on again.

"Must be the handle of the vase," I said over the clatter.

Joey looked at me like I was stupid. "Of course it's the handle. Maybe we can get at it through the bag."

The top of the bag hung from the handle on a hook. I slipped it off. There was a long clamp that held the top of the bag shut, and I slipped that off too. The vacuum cleaner was still running.

You'll never believe what happened. It caught us both by surprise. There was this big *whoooooosssh* of wind out of the bag, and dust blew all over the room. It was just like a black snowstorm.

I'll admit that, until then, I didn't know anything about how a vacuum cleaner works. I'd never given it much thought, and I don't think Joey had either. Now I know what happened. The air in a vacuum cleaner sucks up the dust and blows it into the bag, where it is captured.

I still think, though, that it was Joey's fault because he didn't turn off the vacuum cleaner.

I was squatting over so I was out of the direct line of fire, but Joey got it right smack in the face. He was sputtering and coughing, and his face was covered with an inch of dust. I turned off the vacuum cleaner, and got him to lie down on the sofa.

The tears rolled down his cheeks, and he managed to gasp that he'd been blinded. That scared me some, and I ran for the medicine chest again. This time I came back with some eye drops.

He couldn't seem to hold his eyes open while I squeezed in some of the stuff, so I finally held them open myself. Then I led him, staggering, to the bathroom. He felt a lot better after he'd washed his face. He said he could see again, even though he squinted some, and kept rubbing his eyes with the bandage on his finger.

We didn't dare use the vacuum cleaner again, so we put it back together, then wiped up as much of the dirt as we could with our dust rags. We did a fine job on the tops of the tables, but the drapes were streaky. This didn't bother me, and I told Joey so. The dust gave the drapes a kind of sunburst effect that really was attractive.

"The birthday cake," said Joey. "We'd better get it in the oven before Mom gets back."

"What kind does she like?"

He thought for a minute. "I guess she likes any kind because she makes all kinds for Dad and me."

We headed for the kitchen and found her recipe book. After looking over all the cake recipes, we chose one that said "Delicious White Cake (lovely to look at . . . luscious to eat)." I found the cake pan while Joey got out all the ingredients and lined them up on the counter top.

"What does this mean?" asked Joey, looking over the recipe. " 'Cream together until fluffy ½ cup shortening and 1⅓ cups sugar.' "

I thought pretty hard. "Well, I suppose it means stir in enough cream to make the stuff fluffy."

We tried putting the shortening and sugar into a bowl and adding some cream, but it just got slushy, with big lumps in it. The more cream we added, the more watery it got, so we started adding more sugar and shortening. That made it thicken up, but it never did get fluffy.

We decided it would be okay anyway.

The next step was to add 2 cups of flour. I held the big canister of flour, while Joey dipped in a coffee cup. And do you know what he did? He overfilled the cup, so he had to knock it against the inside of the canister to tap some of the flour out. I guess he didn't know how hard he was tapping, because he knocked the canister right out of my hand. It thunked against the floor, and flour flew all over the room.

Joey should have known better than that.

We cleaned most of it up and put it back in the canister. Then we added 2 cups to our ingredients, along with some milk and baking powder, like the instructions said.

It was the last step that really gave us fits. The recipe said, "fold in 3 egg whites stiffly beaten." Joey got out another bowl, and I cracked one of the eggs. I tried to pour out the egg white alone, but the yellow ran right out of the shell with it.

Joey got another bowl and another egg, so I tried again. The same thing happened. I don't suppose you can blame the hens, but you'd think somebody would breed chickens that would lay eggs that are all white or all yolk, wouldn't you?

"Strain 'em," said Joey.

It sounded like a good idea. Joey got out his mother's strainer and held it over another clean bowl while I poured in the eggs. We were both surprised when the yolks and whites dripped right through that strainer together. After all, what's a strainer for except to strain?

It was Joey's idea to look through the recipe book again to solve the problem. This time we found a recipe for a "Whole Egg Cake (will melt in your mouth)."

Joey didn't think we should put in the shells, but I disagreed. "It says 'whole egg' cake, doesn't it?"

Finally he saw my point, so we tossed the shells into the bowl, too, and beat the daylights out of the eggs with the electric mixer. I'm sure I was right, because you could hardly see even a speck of eggshell when we'd finished.

"'Fold in,'" said Joey, reading out of the recipe book. "Meaning?"

"I suppose you make kind of a ditch through the rest of the cake, then pour the eggs into the ditch. Then the other stuff will kind of fold in over the eggs."

It sounded like a good guess, so that's what we did, being very careful not to mix the eggs and the other stuff any more than we could help. We put the cake very gently in the oven, and Joey turned the oven up to 350 degrees.

"What shall we make your mother for dinner?" I asked.

Joey looked at the kitchen clock. It said 3:30. "Getting late. Final inspection, then we'll get dinner."

Well, we wandered all through that house, picking up things we'd overlooked before, and adjusting everything on the shelves just so. We couldn't make the beds because the sheets were still in the washer, and there were sizable puddles in all the closets, but otherwise things looked fine.

At least I thought they did until Joey and I met in the living room. Then I happened to look at the floor. There were white footprints coming out of the kitchen and going in every direction. In the living room, they turned to gray, and then black.

We both knew what had happened. The floor in the kitchen was still wet from where we'd thrown the rainy clothes on it. Then Joey had knocked the flour out of my hand all over the floor. What we hadn't managed to sweep up made a kind of flour-and-water paste, and we'd tracked that around. Whenever we went through the living room, the paste picked up the dust that the broken vacuum cleaner had blown all over.

Joey and I looked at those footprints, and we couldn't help laughing. They really didn't look bad—kind of interesting, as a matter of fact. Anyway, with the vacuum cleaner broken there wasn't anything we could do about them.

We drifted back out to the kitchen, and I asked Joey again about dinner.

"A casserole," he said, without any hesitation. I knew what he meant, and why he suggested it. A casserole is everything that's left over, dumped into one dish, so it would be easy to make.

So that's what we did. We didn't even look for a recipe.

Joey cut up the ham into little pieces and threw them into a glass dish. I added some green beans and peas I found in the refrigerator. We chopped up a couple of potatoes and put them in, along with three slices of bologna and some cheese.

"Flavoring," said Joey.

We poured some catsup and barbecue sauce over the top, and I added some stuff labeled "meat tenderizer" just in case the ham was tough. We topped it all off with a couple of stalks of celery that contrasted fine with the catsup.

Actually, it looked very tasty, and if I ever get in the mood for a casserole, which I doubt, I'll try this one.

We slipped the casserole into the oven with the cake. There was something funny about that cake, though. It was beginning to puff up and lop over the sides of the pan, but that ditch still ran right down the middle, and it was a different color than the rest of the cake. I wondered whether the people who published that recipe book knew that there was a mistake in it.

Joey and I sat down in the living room and waited for his mother to come home so we could surprise her. He looked a little strange because he still had a lot of dust right around his neck, his eyes were still watering, and he'd spilled some catsup on his bandage.

We hadn't sat there more than ten minutes, talking about Joey's cousin Gary's cat's kittens, when we heard a car door slam out front. Joey ran out on the porch, and I followed. Mrs. Gootz was just coming up the walk with Mrs. Filbert.

Joey's mother took one look at his bandaged finger and almost fainted. "Joey!" she exclaimed, running up the front steps. "What happened?"

Well, the bandage did look pretty bad with all that catsup smeared across it. Joey finally calmed down his mother, and by then Mrs. Filbert was standing on the porch too.

"Happy birthday again, Mrs. Filbert," said Joey, and I said the same thing.

"Thank you, boys. It really has been a fine birthday." She smiled proudly. "Look at what Ronald gave me this morning." Ronald is what she calls Tubs.

She had stopped at home, and now was wearing a gold bracelet that really did have some class, though I hated to admit it.

"I'll bet you have a surprise for your mother too, Joseph." She was trying to find out Joey's gift for his mother.

"Yeah," said Joey. "A surprise."

"Come on in, Edna," said Joey's mother. "I'll get that book you wanted to borrow."

Before we could do anything about it, both of them walked into the living room. Joey's mother let out a kind of a gasp when she saw the floor and the drapes. "Good heavens! What's been going on here?"

Joey started to answer, but then Mrs. Gootz said, "Just a minute. Wait until I get the book for Edna." She obviously wanted to get rid of Mrs. Filbert, and so did we. After all, our birthday surprise was for Joey's mother, and we didn't want to share it with Mrs. Filbert.

Mrs. Gootz got the book, and sort of pushed Mrs. Filbert toward the door, but in a nice kind of way. Mrs. Filbert looked at Joey and me, sniffing like she does when she disapproves, and finally left.

Joey's mother didn't say a word. She just walked through the house, looking at everything—in the kitchen, the basement, even in the closets. We followed her. Finally she sat down in the living room. Her fingers were curled into tight little balls.

"I have to go home for supper now," I said.

"Maybe you can help clean up this mess tomorrow," suggested Joey's mother.

I brightened up. "Sure. I'll be over in the morning." Then an idea struck me—really a very generous thought. "I usually get fifty cents an hour for odd jobs, but tomorrow's work is free. It's on me. Kind of a present for you. Happy birthday, Mrs. Gootz!"

Finally she smiled, just a little, and I knew that eventually everything would be all right.

On the front steps was Mr. Gootz's missing shoe. Mrs. Fenneman's yellow dog must have got tired of playing with it.

Just as I headed down the walk I smelled something burning, and heard Joey shout, "The birthday cake!"

I ran for home.

4

Read This Chapter by March 15. You May Find Some Ideas That Will Be Helpful a Little Later.

This chapter is all about a particular holiday—an important one.

Which holidays are important to a kid? I mean, which ones are really *fun*?

Anybody would guess Christmas right off the bat. And a kid's birthday. But do you know which holiday comes in third, at least with me and a lot of other kids? Thanksgiving? Nope. Mother's Day? You must be kidding. Children's Day? Don't be ridiculous; every kid in creation knows that Children's Day is a complete bust.

April Fools' Day!

Now, *there's* a holiday! In some ways, April Fools' Day is a lot more fun even than Christmas or your birthday.

The trouble with most people is that they leave April Fools' Day until the last minute. Then they can't think of anything to do except tie knots in shoelaces, nail somebody's shoes to the floor, or put sugar in the salt shaker.

Really, you've got to begin thinking about April Fools' Day a couple of weeks ahead. This gives you plenty of time for planning and getting the supplies for whatever you've decided to do.

Even if I say so myself, Joey and I are among the world's best April Fools' Dayers. We've learned the secret: the simpler the trick, the better. We work pretty hard to come up with a good, simple idea.

Like the time a few years ago, when we sneaked into school on April Fools' Day Eve with one of Betts's chickens. There's a secret way of getting into the school, and every boy learns it in the third grade. It's kind of a sign, among us, that a boy belongs to the gang, instead of being one of the little kids.

Anyway, we got into our own classroom without much trouble, although we got our clothes a little dirty doing it. I was carrying the chicken. We opened Miss Burney's right-hand desk drawer—the one that sticks—put in a note that said "April Fool!" tossed in the chicken, and slammed shut the drawer. There was an awful squawk from inside for thirty seconds. Then silence. Any chicken will go right to sleep as soon as you put it in the dark, which sometimes is convenient.

That year Miss Burney was in charge of the playground before school, and she had to make sure that all the balls, bats, and jump ropes were brought in. That meant all of us kids were in our seats before she came into the room.

Joey and I opened books and pretended to be studying. Miss Burney finally opened the door, walked across the room, and sat down at her desk.

I'm telling you, the suspense was terrible. I thought she'd *never* open that drawer. We got through spelling and geography, and there wasn't a peep from the chicken. Finally we put our geography books away and got ready for arithmetic. That's when she reached for the drawer.

Better than anybody else, Miss Burney knows that her right-hand drawer sticks. She gave it a jerk, and the drawer came flying open.

I guess you'd say the chicken was jerked out of a sound sleep. It let out a tremendous squawk, and flew right up in Miss Burney's face. She screamed bloody murder, and as soon as she screamed, all the girls in the room started screaming too.

The door burst open and in came Mr. Schultz, the principal. The chicken was fluttering all over the room. It landed on Gertrude Blasco's head and got its claws tangled in her long hair. Even before it flew off, Gertrude started bawling.

Mr. Schultz opened his mouth and shouted, "Be

calm, children!" Just then the chicken flew past his face and he threw up his arms to protect his glasses.

Well, it took ten minutes to catch the chicken and calm everyone down. Mr. Schultz finally got hold of the chicken by the legs, and all the kids went back to their desks.

Joey looked at me and grinned. It had been a pretty good April Fools' joke, all right.

Last year we pulled an even better trick. Early in February, there was a big debate in Fairfield over whether to build a new waterworks. It was a hot and heavy issue at the time. Everybody was mad at everyone else, and everyone was bringing around petitions to sign.

You know what a petition is. It's a statement for or against something. People are asked to sign it. A lot of signatures are supposed to prove that a lot of people are for or against something.

Well, Joey noticed that when the petitions were being taken around, nobody really read them before signing. They just automatically signed when the bringer-arounder explained whether the petition was for or against.

I told you Joey was crammed full of ideas right up to his eyeballs. All those petitions gave him a great idea for an April Fools' joke. Best of all, we had plenty of time to plan it.

I imagine you can guess—at least part—of what happened. By March 15 about ten other kids had been sworn to secrecy and knew our plans. We went in a body to visit Mike Summers at his office because we needed the mimeograph machine that he uses to send out bulletins to farmers. He's the County Agent. I figured, because he was Betts's boyfriend, he might help.

"Will you pay for the mimeograph paper?" That was his first question.

We scrounged up 29 cents between us for the paper.

"What are you going to use the mimeograph machine for?" That was his second question. We swore Mike to secrecy, and then told him our plans. By the time we had finished, he was grinning like a jack-o'-lantern.

"Great!" he said, slapping me on the back. "Sure I'll help!"

He typed up the petitions so they looked official. There was space for fifty signatures on each petition, and we gave one to each of our ten kids.

We had five days to go until April 1.

You'd be amazed at how easy it is to get people to sign something without reading it. We'd just say, "Will you sign this petition, Mr. Blaine?" Or, "Here's another of those petitions for you to sign, Mrs. Morgan." Lots of times, people would sign without even asking what the petition was for. If they did ask, we'd just say, "For the kids of Fairfield," which in a way was the truth.

I must have asked exactly fifty-one people to sign,

because old Mrs. Jacobsen was the only one who got out her glasses and actually read the petition. Naturally I let her in on the secret, and wouldn't let her sign. She was laughing so hard the tears came when I walked out the door.

"Good for you!" she shouted after me.

On March 30 we had five hundred signatures, and that included a big share of the adults of Fairfield. Joey and I took them over to see Mr. Grumbley, who runs the *Gazette,* the weekly Fairfield paper. He knows me because I'm his delivery boy, in addition to delivering the *Centerville Times* every day.

Mr. Grumbley has a very glum face—almost a mean one—but he isn't that way at all. He listened to what we had to say, then looked at us sternly over the top of his glasses. I thought maybe we'd goofed in showing him the petitions until he started to grin. His face looked like it was about to shatter into small pieces. "Of course I'll do it!" he said, laughing. "It's the best news story around Fairfield in ten years!"

The weekly issue of the paper was due the next afternoon. That would make it April Fools' Eve. The timing wasn't quite on the button, but it was the best we could do.

The next afternoon I could hardly wait to get to the *Gazette* office and pick up my papers. Mr. Grumbley was there waiting for me. My papers were lying on the table in a batch, upside down. I pulled off the top copy while Mr. Grumbley watched, grinning.

The big headline across the top of the paper said:

LOCAL CITIZENS OVERWHELMINGLY FAVOR
CHILDREN'S PETITION.

Beneath it was the article—if you can call it that. There were only two sentences, then a copy of our petition:

> Almost all Fairfield adults signed a petition distributed this week by the town's children.
>
> A copy of the petition, and the names of those who signed, follows:
>
> We, the undersigned, the adults of Fairfield, agree that we are foolish to sign anything without reading it; that our children are superior to us in wit and intelligence; and that as a token of our admiration for them we will do their chores for one week, and allow them to sleep as late as they wish on weekends.

This was followed by more than two columns of names, printed alphabetically. Right after the last name was printed:

> April Fool! (*Signed*) The Kids of Fairfield.

Well, it caused more excitement around town than the plane that had to make an emergency landing in Muller's pasture. After the adults got over their embarrassment, most of them took it fine. After all, the list of signers included almost everyone in town, even Mayor Pitney.

Some of the kids even got out of doing chores for a week. Not me. Even though Pop signed the petition, he said he'd been fooled into it, and no youngster was going to take advantage of him.

He talks that way sometimes, but he doesn't mean it. Very often.

This year we wanted an April Fools' joke that was completely different, and we wanted to play it on Miss Gillam.

Whenever anybody in school causes trouble, all the other teachers either pretend nothing has happened, or get mad as all get-out. Miss Gillam *does something*, and none of us can ever figure out what it will be. That's why we'd rather play tricks on her than on any other teacher.

Our big idea for an April Fools' joke hit us on a Saturday about the middle of March. Pop had told me to clean out the tool shed. Joey was helping, and while we were working we were trying to figure out a good April Fools' stunt. We thought until our brains were scorching hot, but couldn't seem to come up with any good ideas.

Then suddenly Joey hollered. He was sweeping, over in the corner. I ran over to see what was the matter. He pointed the broom at a big spider web, one of the biggest spider webs I've ever seen.

"That's it!" he shouted. "That's our idea!"

"What is?" I asked, feeling dumb.

"We'll spider-web the schoolroom!"

The idea hit me like a sandbag. This could be our greatest production yet!

During the next ten days we secretly talked to every kid in our schoolroom. Every one of them saw what a great idea it was right away. Even Tubs Filbert said he'd help as long as nobody told his mother.

With only two days to go, I talked by phone with Milly Morrison, who had the measles. She agreed to help. Milly really was the key to the plan, although all she had to do was make a phone call to Miss Gillam.

I don't know whether Miss Gillam noticed anything different about the kids on April Fools' morning. Most of the lunch boxes were stuffed with kite string, wrapping twine, even spools of heavy thread. Sophie Flynn had about two miles of yarn left over from her mother's knitting. It was wrapped around her stomach under her dress, and she looked like she'd gained twenty pounds overnight. Jim McCleary carried in a big package that morning, and told the teacher he had to deliver it downtown after school. Inside the package was half a spool of baling twine.

The Aldrich twins couldn't find anything but their mother's clothesline, so they brought it, fastened up inside their pants legs. They walked like they had two broken legs. I mean, each leg on each side of each of them was broken. Well, you know what I mean.

We were too excited to do much schoolwork that morning. It was a beautiful sunny day, and about all we could do that first hour was gaze out the window and hope everything would go off like clockwork.

Right on the button at ten o'clock Mr. Schultz poked his head in our room, and said, "Milly Morrison is on the phone, Miss Gillam. She'd like to ask you some questions about the assignments this week."

Miss Gillam put Minnie Shugelmeyer in charge of the class before she headed for the school office.

As soon as the door closed, we sprang into action. We figured that we had five minutes at the most. Every kid in the room, except Sophie Flynn, tossed his or her wad of string on the floor at the front of the room. Sophie disappeared into the coat closet and came out ten seconds later with that tremendous wad of yarn.

Then everybody went back to his seat except Joey and me and Jamie Peterson.

I sprang after a ball of string like a wildcat after a field mouse, and tied the end to the leg of a desk. Then I wound it around the desk, tossed it over the light fixture, across the map of Asia, then wound it a dozen times around the Aldrich twins from top to toe. Meanwhile I could hear Joey doing the same thing on the other side of the room. Whenever we'd come to the end of a ball of string, Jamie would be right there with a new one, ready to tie on.

You'd never believe how fast that spider web grew. It went around each kid, up and down the aisles, to the pictures on the walls, and back to Miss Gillam's desk.

Within four and a half minutes, which was the time we'd allotted to the job, that room, every desk, and every kid in it were so thoroughly spider-webbed that nothing could move. As a matter of fact, you could hardly *see* anything through that web.

Joey and Jamie and I had left secret routes open, so we could get to our own desks. The other kids were urging us on, but finally I glanced at the wall clock and shouted "Stop!" I tied off the string and crawled under and over the spider web until I reached my desk. Joey and Jamie were doing the same thing.

Milly Morrison had sworn she could keep Miss Gillam tied up on the phone for five minutes. Then we expected Miss Gillam to walk into the room. We'd holler "April Fool!" and she'd see the joke.

After that (and this was our master plan) we wouldn't have to do any work for the rest of the morning because it would take us that long to unspider the web, or unweb the spider, or whatever you want to call it.

So there we were, all tied to each other and to the desks and the maps and the globe and the lights and the bookshelves and everything else so we couldn't even move.

Then Miss Gillam opened the door and walked in.

"April Fool!" we all yelled at once, from the middle of the web.

Well, she took one look and burst out laughing.

What I didn't understand was that she was still laughing when she walked right back out the door again. I couldn't believe that she would report us to Mr. Schultz, but that's what it looked like.

Our own laughing gradually died away, and then

the tension began to build. Everybody started blaming me and Joey for something that hadn't even happened yet. We honestly didn't feel that we'd done anything wrong, but Joey and I couldn't imagine why Miss Gillam would turn right around and walk out. The longer she was gone, the higher the tension.

Then it happened.

Not many adults know what goes on inside a kid when the fire-alarm bell rings, but maybe Miss Gillam did. It's sort of a built-in reaction, like jerking your hand away from a hot stove, or blinking your eyes when a line drive comes off somebody's bat straight for your head.

Anyway, kids go through so many fire drills that when that bell starts ringing they're on their feet and headed for the door in a split second.

They don't *think*. They *act*.

And that's what happened on April Fools' Day. Except that we all ended up on the floor, completely snaggled in our own spider web. Honest to Pete, I couldn't move. When Jamie tried to crawl away, it tightened a piece of heavy yarn around my neck. One of the Aldrich twins shouted at me to get off his left ear. Girls were shouting, desks were toppling, and fists were just beginning to fly when the door opened.

And Miss Gillam walked in, still laughing.

It grew instantly quiet, and she said in that low voice of hers, the voice that everyone can hear so much clearer than some of the loudmouth teachers around school, "April Fool, class!"

Then we started laughing too. The whole class really was tied into knots. Meanwhile she walked over to the window and looked out at the bright April sunshine flooding the school grounds.

When she turned back, she said, "It's such a nice day that Mr. Schultz has decided to give the rest of the classes free time outside, for the rest of the morning, as long as the fire drill took them out there anyway. I think I'll join them. April Fool, class!"

And out she walked.

I looked across the floor at Joey. "April Fool!" I gurgled at him, meanwhile trying to untie the Aldrich family clothesline that was strangling me.

5

I'm One of the Best Spellers in the State.

Almost every kid has a specialty—something he does better than anyone else. Like Marty Slinger is the fastest runner in school; the Aldrich twins can play tunes by thumping their two heads with drumsticks; and Billy Herbst lives in an old red caboose. (The caboose isn't exactly a specialty, but it does set Billy apart, so everybody envies him.)

My specialty is spelling.

You may not believe that. Ordinarily a kid that gets into as much trouble as I do is a lousy speller, but I'm one of the three best spellers, for my age, in Jasper County—and probably in the state.

It's funny. I can spell words that I never even heard of before. Early this year, when we were practicing for the spelldown, I spelled words like *purblind,* and *neuralgia,* and *gesticulate* without even knowing what they meant.

I have a hunch that people are either good spellers from the day they are born, or they'll never be really good spellers no matter how hard they study. I don't mean kids shouldn't study. But nobody ever became a champion speller that way. Good spelling is something that's born in you, like an appendix on the wrong side, or webbed toes.

I suppose, if I had my choice, I'd rather be a fast runner, or live in a red caboose, than to be a natural born speller. But in Fairfield, spelling is certainly a good thing to be good at.

Our state has an annual spelldown championship. It's run almost like the state basketball tournament, except it's for younger kids.

Each grade school selects its three best spellers. They meet the other grade-school teams in their town to determine the town championship team.

This team then goes on to the county meet, and the regional meet. If it's still a winner, it becomes one of the "Elite Eight." These are the eight best teams in the state, and they go to the capital for the finals. In our state, the finals are televised and the kids who compete become real celebrities. The newspapers run articles about them, and everybody talks about whether Billy Bienfang of Center City spells best under tension, and whether Sally Brooks is weak on her plurals.

Last year I made the Harding School team even though I was a grade behind the other two kids on it. We won the town championship, but got wiped out in the county spelldown. Four-Eyes Fisher spelled *presidency* with a "t." I could have busted his lip wide open. I'll bet I could have gone on to the state finals without making a single mistake if Four-Eyes hadn't goofed.

This year I won a place on the Warren G. Harding Grade School team again. That was in January. The team consisted of me and Minnie Shugelmeyer and Beany Martin. For years, Minnie has been the second-best speller in Harding School, with Beany not far behind. It looked to me like we had a fine chance to get into the "Elite Eight" this year, and maybe even to win the state championship.

We zipped through the Fairfield spelldown when somebody on the Taft team missed the last "e" in *sincerely*. When that happened, I sincerely felt that I could orbit the moon without a spaceship.

We won the county title when I spelled *uncharacteristic* correctly after a kid on the Dover team missed it. So now we were heading for the regional meet in Center City, where we'd be up against Spillville. Ah, Spillville!

By this time the tension around town was building

up. It isn't often that a little town the size of Fairfield has an opportunity to beat the big cities at anything. All of a sudden, I was the most popular kid in town—at least one of the three most popular. Whenever I'd walk downtown, Doc Jenkins would holler "parsimonious" or "sacrilege" at me, and I'd rip off the spelling. Mr. Holmes gave me a free ice cream cone (one dip) every time I walked past the drugstore, and offered me double-dippers if we won the regional spelldown.

It was pretty pleasant for me, walking around Fairfield during those few days. I had a good thing going, and I wanted to keep it that way, at least through the regional meet.

On Saturday morning, with only a week until the regional, I met Joey on my way downtown for my free ice cream cone. It was a cold day, with a March wind whistling down from the north, whirling whiffs of snow like ghosts along the sidewalk. Joey had just bought a new airplane kit and asked me to help him put it together. It seemed like more fun than getting an ice cream cone on a day like that, so I went along to his house.

Down in the basement, we pulled a couple of stools over to the workbench.

"Getting nervous?" asked Joey.

"About what?"

"Regional spelldown."

"Nope. Why should I get nervous? Just another old spelldown. We'll win it."

"Lots of excitement. Around town, I mean." He picked up a wing and glued it to the fuselage.

"Yeah. I wish there was some way we could build it even higher."

Joey thought for a minute. It seemed to be a challenge to him. "Maybe there is."

"What do you mean?"

"I dunno. Big parade. High school band. Fire the American Legion cannon. Something like that."

"Spell *cannon,*" I said, without even thinking.

Joey left out one of the "n's." He never was much of a speller.

I pointed out his mistake, and then reminded him that I was in an awkward position. I couldn't suggest that people hold a big parade to honor me.

"True," said Joey. "Besides, it's the wrong time of year for a parade." Carefully he put down the airplane and looked at me. "Let's get this straight. What are we really trying to do?"

I thought for a moment. "Remind the whole town that next Friday night we'll be meeting Spillville in the regional spelldown."

"Remind the town," repeated Joey, frowning. Finally he looked up. "The water tower."

As I told you before, Joey is full of ideas. This one was a knockout.

There's a hill right in the middle of Fairfield, with our old water tower on top of it. The tower is so high that I can see it from my bedroom window, and we live all the way out on the edge of town. Everybody else in town who even glances in that direction can't help but see the tower.

I knew right away what Joey meant. Nobody knows when it started, but there's a custom around Fairfield to paint messages on the water tower. If you look closely you'll find things like "Class of '54" and "Beat the Earlville Dolphins" and "Support the Red Cross Drive" and "BUGGSY JOINER LOVES MARY PITTS."

"Big letters," said Joey, still thinking aloud.

"Mighty big," I said. "Otherwise they'd be lost."

"About as tall as us."

"What color?" I asked.

Without answering, Joey went upstairs. I followed. We gazed out of the living room window at the water tower, up on top of the hill. It was like a big black cylinder.

"Bright orange," said Joey, finally answering my question. "The new kind, that looks like it's fluorescent."

"Spell *fluorescent*," I said.

He made a real mess of it, so he hit me.

I rubbed my shoulder. "Where could we get some?"

"Hardware store. I've seen it there."

"Let's go see how much it costs," I said.

Mr. Lynn was on a stepladder, reaching up to straighten a shelf. You never know whether his hearing aid is turned on or not, so you don't know whether to shout or speak in a regular voice.

I tried shouting. "Hello, Mr. Lynn!"

He dropped a box of brass screws, and almost fell off the ladder. Quickly he reached into his shirt pocket. I knew he was turning down his hearing aid. He looked at us, then climbed down the ladder.

"You don't have to shout," he said. He grinned. "Hello, Joseph. And Peter. How's the great speller?" Mr. Lynn always uses everybody's full first name.

"Fine," I said. "That's what I want to talk to you about."

"What?" he said. "Speak up. I can't hear you. Don't be bashful, laddy. Speak up and make yourself heard."

"I wanted to talk to you about the spelldown," I said in a louder voice.

"Oh. The spelldown. Lots of excitement about that, laddy."

"Mr. Lynn, do you have any of that bright orange paint that seems to glow in the sun? They use it for highway signs."

"Sure do. Follow me." He led the way to the paint shelves, and pulled out a one-gallon can.

"How much is it?" I asked.

"Pretty expensive," he said. "Nine dollars a gallon."

That shook me up. I guess my face showed it.

"What do you want it for, Peter?" he asked. "Maybe we can find something cheaper that will do just as well."

"I don't think so. This kind would be best, Mr. Lynn. It's—well—it's for some signs we're making for the spelldown."

Mr. Lynn thought for a moment. "Tell you what. Miss Gillam is a fine teacher, and if she has told you to make signs, I guess you'd better do it."

I didn't say a word.

"I'll give you the regular school discount. One-third off."

"That's six dollars," I said.

"Bright boy," said Mr. Lynn. Then he must have seen the expression on my face. "Now in addition to that, I'd like to make a small contribution to the spell-down team's success. I think I could afford to pay half the cost of that paint."

"Three dollars," I said, still frowning.

He looked at me sharply. "You laddies don't have even three dollars?"

We shook our heads.

He thought for a moment. "I'll tell you what. I sure can use some help around here. I've been so rushed I haven't had time to clean up the place."

He hadn't had a customer since we'd walked in the door, but I didn't mention that to him.

"You boys help me clean up this section of shelves, and you can take out your wages in trade. Three dollars' worth. Seems to me that's a fair proposition."

"Spell *proposition,*" I said to Joey.

But it was Mr. Lynn who answered. "P–r–o–p–" he began.

That afternoon, back down in Joey's basement, we tried some of the paint on a board. You'll never believe how bright it was. Honest to Pete, it was almost as though it was on fire.

Joey grinned across the board at me. "Tonight. What time shall we start?"

"Let's make it about 8:30," I said. "That's late enough so no one is likely to see us. We should be able to get the whole job done within half an hour or so." Then I asked him the question that I should have been asking myself. "You sure you aren't scared, or anything?"

"I'll make it," said Joey.

"Then we'd better do some planning. Get a couple of pencils and some paper."

We wrote out the message we were going to paint on the water tower. At first we figured that I'd start at the beginning of the message and he'd start with the last letter, and we'd work toward each other. When we tried it on paper, it didn't turn out so good because Joey couldn't spell backwards. So we changed places, and I began at the end.

This didn't work so good either, because we met too soon in the middle, and part of the letters overlapped.

Finally we discovered a system that would work fine, even up on the water tower. I took the first letter and Joey took the second. We did them at the same time, in order to do the job as fast as possible. Then we both moved over, and I took the third letter while he took the fourth. That way our spacing would always be even, and I could keep my eye on Joey. I didn't trust his spelling under the best of conditions, and I had no idea what he'd do on a high water tower.

We found another brush, and an empty coffee can. We put part of the paint in the can.

"You'd better dress plenty warm," I said to Joey as I was leaving. "It's going to be cold on top of that tower."

I couldn't eat much supper that night. It wasn't that I was excited, just that there was a lump in my throat that wouldn't let much food through.

Mike Summers was there, sweet-talking Betts. She invites him every Saturday night, so it's the best meal she fixes all week. That night we had meat loaf, with parsnips sliced thin as a penny and fried crisp, the way I like them best. But I couldn't even force down many parsnips.

Mike noticed what was happening. "Hey, Pete," he said, "you'd better eat more than that. You'll never get to be a volunteer fireman unless you keep up your strength." Mike is always kidding me about my big ambition to be a volunteer fireman. This year he's a lieutenant on the force.

The firehouse in Fairfield is up near the top of the hill, just a block from the water tower. Mrs. Peabody lives right next door, and the town pays her to direct the firemen. When somebody calls in a fire, she gets their name (she knows everybody in town), then runs out and rings the big bell in front of the fire station.

All the volunteer firemen are duty-bound to run to

the fire station. The first two firemen open the big door and drive the fire truck wherever Mrs. Peabody says.

"I'm just not hungry tonight, Mike," I said.

Mike's one of the nicest guys I've ever known, even though he's sweet on Betts. He works as County Agent. What he likes best is working with wild creatures. He knows how to care for an orphaned kit fox, and how to keep pheasants alive through a hard winter.

"How would you like to go down by the creek in Springer's Woods tomorrow and watch that new beaver family?" he asked.

"Fine," I said, already looking forward to it.

About 8:15 I put on my heavy jacket and said to Pop, "I'm going over by the library." This wasn't exactly a lie, because we had to walk by the library to get to the water tower.

"Be back by nine. You hear?"

"Sure, Pop."

It was lighter out than I thought it would be—a clear night, without a cloud in the sky. A three-quarter moon was hanging over Fairfield. Have you ever noticed how much colder it is, in the winter, when the sky is clear? By the time I got to Joey's house, I'd already pulled the flaps on my cap down around my ears, turned up my collar, and put on my mittens.

Joey was waiting on his back porch. He'd made some kind of excuse to his folks too. We sneaked out to the shed by the alley, where Joey's father stores his ladders and lawn mower. We'd hidden the cans of paint and the brushes there that afternoon. We picked them up, and started toward the water tower.

Neither of us said a word until we were about halfway up the hill. The wind was in our faces, and I was getting mighty shivery by then. I could feel the paint sloshing around in the can, just from my shakes.

I glanced over at Joey. "You sure you want to do this tonight?"

When he didn't say anything, I went on, "I'll bet you're pretty cold. That jacket isn't as heavy as mine."

Still he didn't say anything.

"Maybe you'd rather wait till tomorrow night. Might be warmer by then."

He finally said, in the voice you use when somebody steps on a sore toe, "If we're going to do it, let's do it, instead of talking about it."

I noticed right away he had put an "if" in there. He probably didn't want to go through with it. I stopped on the sidewalk. "What's the matter, Joey? You getting cold feet?"

"Nope. You're the one who's talking about quitting."

That wasn't true. I was just cold, that was all. I thought we might be more comfortable another night. "Come on," I said, "let's get it over with."

We passed the firehouse, which was dark as a tomb. The water tower stands in the middle of three vacant lots. We sneaked past Mrs. Peabody's lighted windows, and out across the vacant land toward the water tower.

There are four legs that hold up the water tank. One of the legs is built like a ladder. We stopped beneath that one, and I looked up. The moon was hidden behind the tank, and gave the whole tower a kind of a halo. I'd never realized before how high that water tower was. It looked like the ladder stretched up through the night air all the way to Kingdom Come.

"Who's going first?" asked Joey.

Right away I was sorry he'd beaten me to the question, because it meant that I'd *have* to go first.

"I will," I said.

Joey opened his can of paint with a screwdriver he'd brought along. I was carrying the coffee can, and it didn't have any lid or even any handle. That was going to make it awkward. I put the paintbrush in my pocket, pushed my collar a little higher, and balanced the coffee can on the palm of my right hand. I put my foot on the bottom rung and stepped upward.

That first step was like starting up the first hill of the roller coaster over at Center City; you know you'll never be able to stop until you're through.

My right elbow was crooked around the right side of the ladder, so I could hold myself in against the ladder, and at the same time balance the can of paint. I went up about fifteen steps, sliding that right arm up with each step. Then, without looking down, I called, "Okay. You can start up now." For some reason I wanted Joey close to me.

I could hear him start up the ladder. As soon as he was so close I could hear his breathing, I started climbing again. Within a few steps I found out that he could climb faster than I could because of the handle on his paint can.

I went up about twenty-five more rungs of the ladder, then stopped to rest. He was right behind, and stopped with his hand on the same rung as my feet.

"What's wrong?" he asked.

"Nothing. Just resting."

He didn't argue, so we hung there two, maybe three minutes. By now we were high above Mrs. Peabody's roof, although I didn't look down. The wind was fresh up there, chilling my nose. It's funny how everybody has something that gets cold first. On me, it's my nose.

"Are we going on up, or spending the night here?" Joey finally asked.

He'd done it to me again, with another question. Now I *couldn't* be the one to suggest we go back down, which had been in the back of my mind because it was so cold up there. I didn't even answer; just started climbing again.

I'd climbed maybe thirty more steps, and was getting an awful sinking sensation—really a scaredy-cat feeling—in the center of my stomach, when it happened.

A gust of wind came tearing out of the north so suddenly that it started pushing me right around the ladder. Without thinking, I squeezed the right side of the ladder with my right arm, and the movement was so sudden that the can of paint went slipping out of control. I knew better than to try to get it back again, so I just let it go and grabbed the ladder with both hands.

There was a *clonk* below me, then a sputtering gasp. Silence.

"You still there, Joey?" I asked.

"Yeah. I'm here." The words were squashed together, like he was trying to talk and keep his mouth closed at the same time.

"That wind knocked the paint out of my hands," I said.

"I know. Hit over head. Paint running down face. Into eyes and mouth."

I thought for a minute. "Do you still have your paint?"

"Yeah."

"Well, you're going to have to go on up and do the job alone, now that I don't have any paint."

"Can't. Can't see. Paint in eyes. Besides, can't get past you."

I'd really outfoxed myself this time. By suggesting that Joey go on up alone, I'd put myself in a position where I'd have to do it myself. I didn't like the idea, but I couldn't see any way out.

"Okay," I said finally. "Hand up the paint."

Joey climbed up until his head was even with my knees. He reached one arm up, and I reached down and grabbed the handle of his paint bucket.

A moment later I heard him scrambling down the ladder to the ground. Believe me, he was moving faster than when he came up.

I started climbing again. It was easier with the handle on the paint can, but I kept thinking about how far away the ground was getting. That didn't help much.

The higher I climbed, the more the wind blew. Maybe it was just my imagination, but it seemed to me that every time a gust blustered out of the north, the whole water tower swayed a little. Even though it was cold, I could feel the sweat running down inside my jacket.

"You still there, Joey?" I called during a rest stop.

"Still here," he said. It sounded like his voice was coming from the bottom of Mr. Miller's old well. "I can barely see you, Pete. You sure are getting high!"

That didn't help a bit, either.

There was a long silence, then his words floated up: "You only have a little farther to go." I noticed he was seeing pretty good for a guy with paint in his eyes.

My knees were shaking, but I'd come this far and I wasn't going to quit now. I'd been keeping my eyes on the ladder, right in front of me, instead of looking up or down. Now I risked a glance up. Sure enough, there was the base of the water tank only a few feet above my head.

I took a deep breath, and began climbing again. Those last fifteen rungs were the scariest of all. Then, suddenly, my eyes were even with the bottom of the tank. I'd made it!

The ladder went right on up the tank itself, so I

took a few more steps. As I passed the base of the tank, I could see by the moonlight that a narrow steel ledge, no more than a foot wide, ran all the way around the base of the tank. When my feet were even with the ledge, I stopped. Hanging on with one arm, I reached down and placed the bucket of paint on the ledge.

The wind was gusting stronger than ever, tearing the breath right out of my mouth. I was shivering, and it wasn't all from the cold and the wind.

I was still thinking pretty clearly, though, and figured that the little platform was for repairmen to use if they had to work on the water tank. Therefore there must be some kind of railing around the tank that I'd never noticed from the ground. I swung my hand out in a big circle, feeling the surface of the tank. Sure enough, there was an iron railing that ran around the tank, about as high as my chest.

My teeth were chattering and my arms were shaking so much that I could hardly hang onto the railing. With my toe I shoved the can of paint about a foot or two farther around the tank, then stepped out on the narrow platform.

Scared? Man!

Somehow I managed to get the paintbrush out of my hip pocket. Hanging onto the railing with my left hand, I reached down with the brush and stabbed it blindly in the direction of the paint. I made a bull's-eye too, because I could feel the end of the brush slobber into the paint. I swung the brush back up in front of my face. I knew I was dribbling paint all over my jacket, but I also knew I had to get the job done in a hurry or I'd *never* get it done.

The moon was still as bright as ever, but because I was on the shadowy side of the water tank, I could hardly see anything. I painted a big "B" in front of my face, but I did it mostly by feel instead of sight. Quickly I dipped the brush again and painted an "E" after the "B."

By then I was getting a cramp in my left hand from holding onto the railing, so I put the handle of the paintbrush in my mouth and hung on with both hands for a while, resting. I could feel the paint running off the brush and down my chin, but there was nothing I could do about it.

"You all right up there?" Joey called, his voice sounding faint and shaky on the wind.

I couldn't answer because my mouth was full of paintbrush.

"Hey, Pete! You all right?" His voice was louder, and there was a frantic note in it.

I took the paintbrush out of my mouth. "Yeah!" I managed to shout. Then, just to get back at him, I said, "You should have come on up. It's really wild. Lots of fun!"

"Still can't see," he called.

Yeah. Sure. . . .

I painted a couple of more letters. I was working my way around the tank, and by now was getting a long way from the ladder. The thought scared me. I wasn't paying much attention to what I was doing, just slamming paint all over so I could climb back down from there.

Well, I won't keep you in suspense. I finally painted the last letter, and by then was so cold and scared that I could hardly move.

And the ladder was all the way around on the opposite side of the tank.

I reached down to put the brush in the bucket, but my sense of timing must have gone bad. I missed the bucket, and the brush went flying off into the darkness.

Without even thinking, I did exactly the wrong thing.

I looked down to see what had happened to the brush!

I think I could have made it back down to the ground if that hadn't happened. Up to that point, I'd been very careful never to look down. Now, suddenly, I was looking at half the houses in town, far below. The black branches of the trees were blowing wildly in the streetlights. In that one glance I even saw Mrs. Peabody open the door and let out her dog. That dog looked no bigger than an ant.

But it was only a glance. Quickly I tilted my head back toward the sky, but it didn't make a bit of difference because my eyes were squeezed shut, and the whole world was going round and round inside my head.

I knew I couldn't move. I was plastered right up against that water tank, high in the sky, and *I couldn't move!*

"Joey!" I hollered.

It came out as a squeak, so I hollered again. "Joey!"

"Yeah?" It seemed as though his voice was even fainter than before.

"I need help!" I shouted. My voice was so shaky I could hardly understand it myself.

"What's the matter?"

"I'm stuck!"

"What do you mean, you're stuck?"

"I—I— My jacket's caught. That's it! My jacket's hooked on something up here, and I can't get it loose. I'm stuck!" I don't really know why I said that, about my jacket.

The silence seemed to last forever. Finally Joey called up, "Pete, what do you want me to do?"

Faintly I could hear Mrs. Peabody's dog yapping at her door below. The sound gave me an idea. "Tell Mrs. Peabody to ring the fire bell!" It came out in kind of a gasp.

There was such a long silence that I was afraid Joey hadn't heard me.

Then, suddenly, the fire bell began to ring. It was a block away and about two million feet down, but the sound came through loud and clear.

Honest to Pete, Fairfield has the greatest volunteer fire department in the world. Within thirty seconds I heard shouts, then the roar of the truck as someone drove it over from the firehouse. There was the screech of brakes as a couple of cars came wheeling up to the curbing in front of the water tower.

My eyes were still squeezed shut, but suddenly I sensed a bright light. I opened my eyes for just a second and the whole town was bright as day. I saw a big orange "N" right in front of my nose, the paint still drippy. Then I shut my eyes again.

There were more shouts, then a long silence, as though everyone had gone away.

Finally Mike Summers' voice came up, loud and clear. "Pete! I'm coming to get you!"

I'd never heard anything that sounded so good in all my life. It made me so brave that I started bluffing again. "My jacket!" I shouted down. "It's hooked on something up here and I can't get it loose. Maybe you can help!"

Mike must have known how scared I was because he talked to me all the time he was climbing the ladder. He talked about a horned owl he'd spotted on the quarry road. He talked about a baby raccoon he'd once raised, and about the best way to gig a frog.

I wasn't paying much attention, though, because I was trying to figure the best way out of this situation. I wasn't quite so scared now, with Mike on his way up. Very carefully I let loose of the railing with one hand, and grabbed the bottom of my jacket. I tried to stuff it behind the railing, like it was caught there, but it wouldn't stay. I was moving my hand over the surface of the water tower, feeling for some kind of a hook I could use for my jacket, when I felt a vibration run along the platform under my feet. Mike had reached the water tank.

"Is that you, Mike?" I asked, which when you think about it is a pretty silly question.

"I'm on my way around to help you," he said. "Just keep calm."

I thought very fast and very hard. Then suddenly I shouted, "Oops!"

Mike must have thought I was falling, because he said sharply, "Pete! What happened?"

"My jacket just came unhooked," I said. By now he was only a few feet away. "Hey, Mike! I'm not stuck any longer!" I said it again, louder, so everybody down below could hear it too. "I'm not stuck any longer!"

Mike didn't say a word about that. By now he was standing right beside me. "I'm going to tie a rope around your chest under your arms, Pete. I'll loop the other end around the railing. Then you and I are going to move around the tower and down the ladder."

Well, we did it that way. I felt lots better with Mike there. On the way down I said, "Funny how my jacket got snagged up there. They ought to fix that, or somebody's liable to get hurt some day."

Mike didn't answer, so I said, "Don't you think so, Mike?"

He let out a little grunt. I didn't know what that meant.

I didn't hear any other sounds on the way down, but just as my foot hit the frozen ground a big cheer went up. It made me mighty proud, and I stuck out my chest. There must have been fifty people at the base of the tower—firemen, their wives, even some kids. I noticed Minnie Shugelmeyer over by the fire truck.

Betts was there, and she sort of grabbed at me like I'd risen from the dead. When she tried to kiss me she got bright orange paint all over her mouth, which served her right.

Joey sidled over to stand beside me, and I took a good look at him for the first time. His cap and one whole side of his face were covered with paint, and it had splashed across the shoulder of his jacket. He looked like he was wearing a bullfighter's cape.

"It must have been awful scary up there, Pete." It was Minnie Shugelmeyer's soft voice. She was standing beside me now.

"Not really." I heard the words slip out of my mouth, so I went on, "High places don't bother me at all. Maybe some day I'll be a high-wire walker in a circus. Some people can't stand to be up high, but I like it. It's a good feeling—"

"Let's see your jacket, Pete," Mike broke in. "Is there much of a rip where you snagged it on the water tower?"

Hard as we looked, we couldn't see any damage to the jacket.

Nor to me, either.

I slept late the next morning. The bright winter sun, slanting in my window, finally awoke me. At least it gave me that fuzzy, warm kind of feeling you get when you first become aware of noises around the house.

All of a sudden I remembered what had happened the night before. I shivered and crawled deeper under the covers. But I couldn't keep my mind off the water tower, no matter how hard I tried.

Finally I sat up in bed and looked out the window.

Honest to Pete, I wanted to crawl right back under the covers. In fact, I wanted to crawl under the whole bed.

The town wouldn't forget Peter Potts, champion speller, for a long time.

Scrawled across the water tower, in big glowing orange letters, was the message:

BEET SPILVILE IN SPELDOWN

6

The Giant Soapbox Racer.

As I said on the first page of this book, it's easy to get into trouble by accident. You wouldn't think anyone could get into trouble just by building a soapbox racer.

They run these soapbox races all over the country every year. The kids build little one-man racing cars, and race them downhill. The winner of the national contest gets a college scholarship and is treated better than the President of the United States, at least in recent years. Joey and I have entered together for three years.

The first year, when Joey won the toss to see who'd

be the driver, his front wheel flew off and hit Mrs. Otto in her bifocals.

The next year, when I was driving, Ted Shaner managed to drop some sand on the front axle. About halfway down the hill the bearings froze and I slammed to a stop like I'd hit a brick wall. Did everybody laugh!

It made Joey and me so mad we sneaked over to the Shaners that night with a dead skunk. We dragged the skunk along the ground all the way around the Shaners' house. The Shaners have a prize hound that can smell a 'coon a long mile away. Well, within two minutes that hound set up such a howl you could hear it clear across Fairfield. I've never heard such a rumpus. Nobody in that end of town got a wink of sleep that night. Too bad a lot of other people had to suffer along with Ted, who started it by throwing sand on my axle.

Anyway, about the giant soapbox racer. One day last summer Joey and I were prowling through the junkyard on the hill out west of town. We found half a dozen old cars, their engines gone and their tops all covered with rust. All of a sudden the idea struck Joey.

"The World's Biggest Soapbox Racer," he said, like he was dreaming.

Now, if there's anything that impresses Joey, it's the World's Biggest anything. He knows all the records too. He'll tell you, for example, that the World's Biggest Human Being was Robert Earl Hughes of Fish Hook, Illinois, who weighed 1,069 pounds. Or maybe, out of the blue, he'll mention that the World's Biggest Ant measures 1.3 inches long, or the World's Biggest Grasshopper has a wingspan of 10 inches.

Joey has a whole book of the World's Biggest records, and he practically knows it by heart.

He has set some World's Biggest records himself, with my help. We once built the World's Biggest Flying Disk. Out of Pop's old windmill. Joey got the bright idea of using just the wind wheel itself as a giant flying disk, like the disks you get free in a box of cereal—the kind that go whirling up and away like a helicopter.

When we were ready for our first flight, the wind wheel was pointed toward the sky, and a belt connected it to Pop's three-horsepower electric motor.

When Joey turned on the motor, that windmill started to turn very slowly, and the belt began smoking. Then the wheel began to pick up speed. Finally the vanes got blurred so you couldn't even see them, and the pipe that was serving as an axle began to shake. There was a weird hollow sound, like a low moan. I got scared and hollered to Joey to unplug the motor, but he was too late. The moan suddenly got louder, and the windmill shot up like a cannon shell.

The big wheel veered toward the house, barely clearing the chimney, and then soared across the highway, moaning all the time like it was in some terrible pain. A half mile and fifteen seconds later it began to lose altitude, and swooped down toward Oostermeyer's oat field. It chopped its way through a new fence and cut down half an acre of oats before it came to a stop.

Joey and I had to repair the fence, but it was worth it. We never flew it again, though. Too dangerous.

Another time Joey got this insane idea that we should build the World's Biggest Yo-Yo. We did. It's six feet in diameter, and the string is made of one-inch nylon rope. We haven't figured out how to test it yet, so it's still out in the shed behind our house just gathering dust.

The yo-yo and the flying disk may explain why I was both tempted and a little leery when Joey suggested we build the World's Biggest Soapbox Racer.

"How would we build it?" I asked doubtfully, looking around the junkyard.

"Well, we can get all the parts off these old cars."

We started investigating and, sure enough, we found everything we needed. The more we talked about the idea, the more enthusiastic I got.

Finally I went home and got some of Pop's old tools while Joey fetched a rope. We began taking apart the old cars.

It took us two afternoons of hard work just to get the parts we wanted. Then we started dragging them out onto the grass-grown road that leads to Route 16. We got the wheels out there all right, and the steering gear. When we tried to move the frame of the chassis, though, we had to call in the Aldrich twins to help. They're big for their age, and what one of them can't lift the other one can.

By Saturday afternoon we were putting the parts together. We fastened the wheel mounts onto the frame of one of the cars. We had to chip in 85 cents apiece to buy four old tires from Schwartz's Garage. After we had mounted the tires on the wheels, we jacked up the frame and slipped on the wheels. Then we installed the steering gear, the shaft, and the steering wheel. Last of all we tied a board across the frame with a rope, and nailed a box onto it for a seat.

What we had was sort of a platform on four wheels, with a steering gear.

Finally we all got behind and pushed. It wouldn't budge.

"What do you suppose is the matter?" asked Joey.

We all stood there thinking. Finally one of the Aldrich twins—I never know which is which—said, "I'll bet we need some grease on those wheels."

I ran home and started searching. All I could find was some castor oil from the medicine cabinet, so I brought it back with me. We doused it all over the wheel bearings.

This time, when we all heaved, the soapbox racer moved. We got her going at a pretty good clip down the grassy road.

I jumped up on the seat. The racer moved down the road sweet as you please. It picked up so much speed that before long I left Joey and the Aldrich twins behind. All of a sudden I found myself turning out onto the highway, and lucky for me, nobody was coming.

Once I hit the pavement, I really started moving. I was right at the top of the hill leading down into Fairfield.

I rolled down the hill, picking up more speed. At first it was great. The wind was on my face and the telephone poles began rolling by at a fast clip. It was then that I discovered that driving a car isn't nearly as easy as it looks. I kept zigging and zagging across the road from one side to the other. The more I tried to stop zigging, the more I'd zag.

Halfway down the hill I saw a pickup truck coming toward me. When I tried to get over on my own side of the road, I ran off the shoulder, so I steered back on again, but this time I went clear over on the other side. The truck driver wasn't any better than I was, because he was zigzagging back and forth too.

Would you believe it, that guy passed me on the wrong side? I'll admit I don't know much about driving, but if I hadn't swerved clear over to the left he would have smacked me head-on. I'll bet they'll take his driver's license away some day. As it was, we passed so close I could have reached out and shaken hands with him if we hadn't both been going so fast. All I saw was a white blur where his face should have been.

That kind of experience is enough to scare anybody. With drivers like that on the road, I figured it was time to stop. It was only then that I remembered. Do you know what I remembered? *Joey Gootz had forgotten to put any brakes on that racer!*

Well, you could have knocked me off that driver's seat with a milkweed pod. I didn't know what to do, and I was picking up speed all the time. By now the air was whistling past my face so fast I could hardly get my breath. As I sailed past our house I saw Betts out of the corner of my eye. She was taking down the wash. When she looked up she dropped the clothes basket and stood there just as still as a statue.

At the bottom of the hill I rolled across the bridge so fast it made a sort of a *fffsssssssssst* in my ears and then was way behind me.

I sailed up Main Street toward the business district. Luckily there weren't many cars on the road, and the ones I saw got out of the way in a hurry. Mr. Moser was starting across the street at the corner of Highland Avenue. He looked up just in time, stood there for a minute trying to decide which way to jump, then sort of fell backwards as if he'd fainted. I ran right over his hat.

By the time I hit the business district I'd slowed down a little, and began to hear people shout.

There's one stop light in Fairfield, and as luck would have it, it was red. I don't believe in running stop signs. I've been a patrol boy at school, and I think that anyone who would run a stop sign would steal chickens. That's why I was so worried about that red light. I could see it getting closer and closer, and thank goodness it turned green just before I got there.

The thing that *really* scared me happened a block beyond the business district. Gurney Phelps and Bill

Sherman had been painting the funeral home, and were just knocking off for the afternoon. They were on their way across Main Street with Gurney's long ladder. When they saw me coming they sort of froze in the middle of the street. I thought that was very foolish of them. That ladder kept getting bigger by the second. At the last minute they dropped it and ran both ways.

Maybe at some time you've hit a ladder with a car. If you haven't, don't ever try it. It felt as though a bomb had exploded under me. I'm telling you, I flew three feet in the air, and would have landed over on the curb if I hadn't managed to hang onto the steering wheel. By then, I knew I *had* to hang on, that it was my job to keep that racer under control.

The ladder slowed me down quite a bit, and as I rolled up the Main Street hill I began to get my breath back. At Third Street I eased to a stop.

You know, I've always thought that if I'd jumped off the seat right then I wouldn't have been in any trouble. I hadn't really done any damage.

But before I had enough sense to get off the racer, it started rolling down the hill again *backward.*

It's hard enough to steer when you're going forward, but all of a sudden I discovered that you have to think *left-handed* when you're driving backward.

Well, I'll have to admit I just couldn't get the hang of it. I kept it under control for half a block, but finally bounced up over the curb and hit the fire hydrant in front of Freeland's Farm Store. Water squirted out of the hydrant like it was coming from a great big water pistol. Luckily Ted Shaner just happened to be walking by, and that geyser of water knocked him right off his feet. I hope he remembered the time he threw sand on my axle.

Judge Manfred had quite a lot to say about modern youth. After the judge's lecture, Joey and I were mighty happy to get off with paying for repairs to the hydrant.

Anyway, Joey says we now hold the record for building the World's Biggest Soapbox Racer. He's written it into his record book too. Right on the first page.

7

This Tells About How Joey and I Threw the Biggest Party in the History of Fairfield.

Betts's wedding reception is another good example of trouble-by-accident. I doubt if Fairfield will ever forget that reception.

I suppose it shouldn't have surprised me to learn that Betts and Mike were getting married, but it did. I found it out one night after I'd gone to bed and turned out the lights. My window was wide open to the summer air, and I was just beginning my last yawn when I heard a rustling noise, then voices in the backyard.

"Here, darling. Let's sit down on the picnic table." It was Mike's voice.

There was a long silence with kind of a squishy sound at the end of it. Then Betts sighed. "I really think we should tell Pop and Pete right away that we're getting married."

Her words hit me like a pile driver. Betts married! I pulled the covers over my head. I still do that sometimes. If you have no family except a sister and a grandfather, and then one of them turns traitor and says she's going off to live with somebody else, you suddenly see a pretty big hole in your life.

"I'm worried about how Pete will react." Betts's voice was muffled, coming at me through Grandma's old quilt. "I'm not going to be easy in my mind until I tell him. I'll do it tomorrow."

"Pete will be all right," said Mike. "He has six weeks to get used to the idea. Anyway, he'll want only the best for you—and that's me!" *Squiiiiiiiisssh.* "You tell him about it tomorrow, and when I see him tomorrow night I'll offer to take him on an overnight fishing trip next weekend."

That sort of brought things back into focus. My first thought had been that Betts was leaving the family. But now I could see that Mike would be coming *into* the family—and he might help me develop a prooster. That's my own word for a cross between a parrot and a rooster. Instead of *cockadoodledoing,* a prooster shouts "Get up!" in the morning. It's my own invention, except that I haven't had time to invent it yet.

Now, Mike would be in the family, and had all the know-how to help me.

Besides, I really *did* want the best for Betts.
I poked my head out from under the covers.

The next morning I was scrubbing the kitchen floor, like Pop had asked me to do, when Betts walked in the door. I really was flattered. Betts has missed only two hours' work at McClennan's in two and a half years, and that was the time I got stuck in the revolving door at the bank. If she left her job just to get me alone, this talk must be pretty important to her. I was still on my hands and knees, and looked up at her.

"Pete, I have something to tell you."

"Yeah. I know. About you and Mike getting married. And you're wondering how I'll react." I started scrubbing the floor again.

"Oh, Pete! You heard us talking!" Suddenly she was on the floor with me, never minding her dress in the soapsuds, looking into my face. "Pete, it's going to be just fine for you. You'll have Pop right here with you, and we've already arranged to rent that little house on Schmidt's farm, just down the road. Mike and I will be your next-door neighbors, and we'll see each other all the time."

I could have faked a few tears to give her a bad time, but I didn't. I just wanted her to be happy. "It's fine with me, Betts. Really, I *am* glad. Now I can spend more time with Mike. Do you suppose I'll catch any fish next weekend?"

She squeezed me, right there on the floor, then stood up. She was halfway through the door when she turned around, a frown on her face. She said, "Aren't you even a *little* bit disappointed about me moving out of this house?"

You figure women. I can't.

It was about two days later that Joey hit me over the head with a baseball bat. Not really a baseball bat. Actually, he hit me over the head with a book called *The Etiquette and Manners of Marriage,* which he'd checked out of the library.

" 'Traditionally,' " he read, " 'the bride and her family pay for the bride's wedding and travel outfits; wedding invitations and announcements; and all reception costs.' "

The bride's family consisted of Pop and me. The thought of a reception was scary. Pop never has liked the society bit, so I knew I couldn't count on him to meet his social obligations. That left only me, and suddenly I felt as exposed as a big toe sticking through a worn-out sock.

I went to Pop and explained the situation. He understood right away. "Go ahead, Pete. You handle everything. I'll tell you a secret. I have fifty dollars squirreled away in a hiding place nobody knows about, just waiting for an emergency to happen to one of you kids. Betts's wedding is more important than any emergency. You go ahead and spend it on this marriage party you're talking about. Give those kids the best. Just let me know when you want the money."

Feeling a little better, I went over and asked Joey

to help plan the party. His eyes sort of glazed over at the challenge. He said, "World's Biggest Wedding Reception!" He went in the house and came back with a pencil and paper so he could make notes.

"Who'll we invite?" I asked. Mentally, I'd already eliminated Ted Shaner and Tubs Filbert.

"The whole town," said Joey firmly.

"Okay," I said doubtfully. "But if we're going to have that many people, *where* can we have it?"

There was a long silence. Then we both said it at the same time. "Oostermeyer's barn!"

Vern Oostermeyer has the biggest barn in four counties. It's absolutely huge. A couple of years ago he gave up farming and rented most of his land to a seed-corn company. All he raises now is half a dozen small goats and the dickens on Saturday night. That leaves his big barn standing idle. He's been a good neighbor, and I was sure he'd let us use it.

"Refreshments?" asked Joey, pencil ready.

If we had to provide refreshments for everybody in town, I could see Pop's fifty dollars going down the drain mighty fast. "Kool-Aid," I said. "That's the cheapest thing we can possibly serve. We can put in twice as much water as we're supposed to."

"A wedding cake?"

We finally decided to ask Mrs. Peabody to bake us eight big layers of sponge cake. She's been famous for her cakes since she won first in the state fair. I figured she'd charge us only for the ingredients. And to save even more money, Joey and I would decorate the cake ourselves.

"What about music?" I asked. "Everybody always dances at wedding receptions."

"Let's get the Wonderful Dirty Socks."

The Wonderful Dirty Socks are a rock group that plays for dances around our part of the state. "They'd charge too much," I said. "Pop's entire fifty dollars would go just for the music."

Joey frowned and grunted. He was thinking up a storm. Finally he said, "The Warren G. Harding Grade School Kazoo Band."

The more I thought about it, the better I liked the idea. The kids in the band would play just for the fun of it.

"Great. Now, what else do they have at weddings and receptions?"

"Rice," said Joey. "Everybody scatters rice."

That was a problem. To do the thing right, with that many people involved, we'd need at least three or four bushels of rice, and we couldn't afford it. Finally I made a decision. "We'll use shelled corn. It's kind of like rice, and I'm sure Mr. Oostermeyer has some corn left over that he'll donate."

Joey wrote down "corn" on his sheet of paper. "Decorations?"

"We'll buy some balloons and streamers."

We were really getting in the swing of this planning now. Actually, it was exciting. It was right then that I remembered something. "I was watching an old movie on television a couple of weeks ago," I said. "There was this rich girl getting married to this rich guy. Right at the end of the reception, which was held on the lawn of a big mansion, they let loose about fifty million doves. It really was a neat sight."

Joey pulled on his left ear, which is a sure sign he's thinking. His left earlobe hangs down more than his right because of that. "We'll get all the farm kids at school to trap every pigeon in every barn loft in Jasper County. We'll release at least fifty million pigeons at this party!" He was getting carried away.

Didn't I tell you Joey was full of ideas?

We worked mighty hard the next few weeks.

Mr. Oostermeyer was happy to donate his barn in honor of Betts, so we cleaned it all out, even the goat pen. We planned to tether the goats up in the loft on the day of the reception. We strung streamers all around, and blew up balloons.

Joey took charge of Operation Pigeons and got the farm kids at school organized. He even arranged to get a dozen tomato crates from the canning factory to store the pigeons until we let 'em fly. The kids had fun outwitting those birds. It wasn't long until the crates were overflowing with them, and it was a problem keeping them properly fed with corn donated by Mr. Oostermeyer. I began worrying about them starving before the reception.

We slung half a dozen bushel baskets full of corn from the roof of the barn. Then we rigged a long piece of binding twine to each basket, so when you gave it a jerk the corn would come spilling out, showering down on the bride and groom below. I gave the Aldrich twins and four other guys in my grade the job of jerking the twine on my signal. Joey figured this would be much more spectacular than just throwing handfuls of rice.

The wedding was planned for seven o'clock at night, with the reception right afterward.

Around noon of Betts's wedding day, Mrs. Peabody delivered eight big layers of sponge cake, each about two feet square, to the barn. When I asked how to make frosting, she told me to use just confectioner's sugar and plain water.

"That's the simplest frosting of all," she said. Those were her very words, and I'll bet she's thought them over many a time since.

By midafternoon we were mixing up a clean washtub full of Kool-Aid, stirring it with a fresh-cut willow branch about four feet long. When it tasted proper enough, Joey rode his bike over to Sullivan's Grocery to get a dozen big boxes of confectioners' sugar for the frosting, while I fetched the biggest mixing bowls in our house. A half hour later he had mixed up three gallons of white frosting that tasted mighty good. We were ready to decorate the cake.

We put one layer of the sponge cake on a card table

that Joey's mother had loaned us, and I smeared frosting all over it with a garden trowel. Another layer went on, with more frosting. Then another.

I really don't know what was wrong with that frosting of Joey's. Everybody knows that frosting is just naturally *sticky,* which is why kids always get in trouble eating it. Maybe Joey put in too much water, or didn't let the frosting stand long enough, or something. Anyway, his frosting was *slippery*—slippery as three gallons of eels. You'd think Mrs. Peabody would have given us a recipe that was sticky instead of slippery.

Maybe I didn't balance the cake quite right, either. Anyway, I was standing on a milking stool, just putting on the top layer when I thought I saw something move lower down. Sure enough, that whole cake was beginning to sloop and slide. The darn thing wiggled like it was alive.

"Joey, toss me that stick!" I hollered, pointing to the long willow branch in the Kool-Aid.

He knew an emergency when he saw one, and flipped the stick from twenty-five feet away. I caught it by one end, and immediately stuck it down through the whole cake from above, like skewering a sword through a bad guy in the movies. The cake stood there quivering on the table for a minute. Then it relaxed, like it was dead.

It looked goofy standing there with layers poking out in all directions and that green willow branch sticking up from the top. Still, it now seemed solid as a rock. Joey's mother had very kindly contributed a little bride doll and a groom doll, so we lashed them to the stick above the cake. They looked like they were about to be burned at the stake.

We had trouble getting the goats up into the loft, but finally we had them tethered there. Then we headed on home to get dressed up for the big wedding —and the reception.

It *was* a big wedding too. Mike and Betts are both mighty well liked around Fairfield. There was standing room only in the church, and some people didn't even get through the front door.

When it came time for Pop to give the bride away, I thought I saw a tear in his eye, but maybe it was only the light reflecting off his glasses. After all the "I do's" and "now pronounce you man and wife's," Mike stuck his head under Betts's veil and gave her a kiss.

Pop doesn't know much about manners, but he has what the preacher once called a warm soul. As soon as the kiss was over he got to his feet and said, "The Potts family—Pete and myself—invite everybody out to Oostermeyer's barn for a wedding reception."

Joey was sitting right next to me. "Here we go," he whispered. "The World's Biggest."

I tell you, Joey and I were mighty proud when we rolled back the barn door and led the bride and groom inside. At that very moment the Warren G. Harding Grade School Kazoo Band struck up the "Wedding

March." They had learned it especially for the occasion, and I must admit that it sounded mighty good coming from eleven kazoos, three pairs of pot lids, and a borrowed snare drum.

Betts really was impressed when she saw what we'd done with the inside of the barn. The balloons and streamers looked mighty pretty in the twinkly light coming from the Christmas tree bulbs we'd strung all over.

Within ten minutes the whole town was there. We had roped off one section of the barn to use as a dance floor, and the kazoos soon were providing the music. Actually, the kids knew only three pieces—"Stars and Stripes Forever," "On Top of Old Smokey," and "Happy Birthday to You." Some of the older folks had trouble dancing to that kind of music, but the kids were having a ball.

Everybody told us how good the Kool-Aid tasted. I happened to see Vern Oostermeyer pour something from a bottle into his first glass of it. It wasn't long before he was dancing across the floor all by himself, and I've hardly ever seen such rhythm.

Mike and Betts seemed to be enjoying themselves, along with everybody else.

Finally after about an hour Betts stood up in front of everybody and announced that she was going to throw her bouquet.

"What does she mean?" I asked Mike.

"It's an old tradition. The bride throws her bouquet backward over her head toward all the unmarried girls.

Whichever girl catches it is supposed to be the next girl to get married."

Well, all the unmarried girls in town older than fifteen got on one side of the barn. Even Miss Toliver was there, and she must be at least sixty-five. I guess she still has hopes. Betts stood across the barn, facing the other way.

Right here I should tell you that Betts has a great right arm, and has been pitcher on the Fairfield Girl's Softball Team for five years. Two of those five, Fairfield won the state championship.

Anyway, Betts really wound up her pitching arm and heaved that bouquet back over her head. It sailed up through the air.

And never came down.

That's right. It never came down.

It really was weird. All the unmarried girls in town were standing there waiting and waiting, and the bouquet never came down.

I looked up and finally solved the mystery. One of the Oostermeyer goats was eyeballing me from the loft while it swallowed the last few lilies of the valley. That goat even ate the ribbon.

I don't know whether it means anything, but I *did* notice she was a female goat. Maybe she's married by now.

I guess Miss Toliver was pretty disappointed.

After all the shouting and laughing about the goat died down, Mike announced that he and Betts were going to cut the cake. I figured the party was coming to a climax, so I gave Joey the high sign—patting the top of my head three times—and he scurried off with all the kids from our grade. Each knew what to do; some grabbed the ropes hanging from the baskets of make-believe rice, and the others stood by the pigeon crates we'd hidden along one wall under an old tarp.

It gives me a funny feeling just thinking about what happened after that. Mike picked up Pop's big butcher knife, and then looked down at Betts. She looked back up at him with a strange little half-smile on her face, and suddenly I remembered, from a long-long time ago, how my mother looked. Then Mike held out the knife, and together they reached up and pushed it all the way down through the cake.

They must have upset that cake's delicate balance, because half of it suddenly was sliding on the slippery frosting in one direction, and the other half was toppling the other way. The stick stayed in the toppling half. The dolls on top swung down in a big arc and hit Minnie Shugelmeyer's little sister on top of the head. She can bawl bloody murder, so she did.

There was a gasp of horror from everyone just as the kazoos struck up the "Wedding March" again. I guess I panicked, seeing what happened to that cake, and I patted my head again.

I don't suppose very many people have ever been hit by a bushel of shelled corn dropped from a height of thirty-five feet. When Joey planned the reception, he figured the corn would scatter all over the place, like tossed rice. Instead, all six bushels came bashing straight down out of the darkness in big globs, like six meteors. One hit Mike and Betts, and another staggered Pop.

At the same moment I heard a big *whoooooooooosh* and the flutter of about a million wings. Joey and I had figured the pigeons would fly in a flock once around the barn, pretty as a picture, just like those doves had done on television, and then fly on out the back door toward their homes. Instead, they were so hungry from being cooped up that they swooped down on the corn and sponge cake like a thousand jet dive-bombers.

It really was an exciting sight. Everyone tried to wave off those crazy birds like they were vampire bats or something just as dangerous. Old Mr. Calhoun swung his cane at a couple of them so hard that he dislocated his shoulder and had to go to the hospital in Center City the next day. It cost him a pretty penny, but he married the head nurse.

After that, for some reason, a lot of people started saying good-bye and heading for home, even though there was still plenty of Kool-Aid left. The kids liked the excitement and didn't want to leave, but the parents had had enough, I guess.

Mike and Betts cornered me. Betts was still brushing corn out of her hair, but she had a smile on her face as big as the moon.

"Pete," she said, "you gave me the greatest wedding

reception any bride ever had. I'll never forget it—and I don't think anyone else in Fairfield will ever forget it, either."

"World's Biggest Wedding Reception," said Joey proudly.

"Indeed it was," said Mike. He slipped his arm around Betts, and looked across at me. "We'll be slipping away now, Pete. You'll have to watch after Pop while we're gone. I know you'll take good care of him."

"I'll try." Maybe my eyes got a little misty. "Have fun in Chicago. And I'm—well—I'm sorry about the corn and the pigeons. That didn't work out so well."

I think Betts's eyes were kind of misty too. She kissed me on the cheek right there in front of everyone. She started to say something, swallowed twice, and walked over to Mike's pickup truck.

Don't you think at least she could have said goodbye?

The next morning Pop and I were sitting in the living room, missing Betts and feeling sorry for ourselves, although neither of us said anything about it.

After a while, Joey came walking in and flopped down in a chair too. Nobody said much. I counted to myself while Grandma's old clock ticked five hundred times.

Suddenly Pop jumped to his feet. "By jabbers, what a man needs at a time like this is a new hobby, and I know what mine's going to be."

That made me curious. "What?"

"French cooking, Pete! I'm going to be a French chef. I'm going down to the library right now and see if they have any French cookbooks. We'll have *truffles* and *escargot* for dinner!"

He stood there, his eyes sparking down at me. I knew what he was trying to do. Pop really *will* try his hand at French cooking, or any other kind of cooking, now that Betts won't be on hand to cook for us. But more important, he was trying to cheer me up.

"How about you, Pete? What are you going to do?" he demanded.

"I dunno."

Joey chimed in pretty quick. "Idea. The clump of four oak trees in the corner of Gilligan's pasture."

"What about it?" I said.

"Old shed on top of the hill."

I nodded again. It was close by the oaks. It hadn't been used for as long as I could remember, and finally last spring had come crashing down in a high wind.

"Get the lumber from the shed. Build a tree house that goes from one tree to another, through four trees. *World's Biggest Tree House!*"

I liked the idea right away. We headed outdoors for our bikes. As I rode away, I looked back at Pop. He was standing on the front porch, grinning and waving at me.

Deep inside, I knew Betts was having the time of her life. And now everything in the world was fine again.